"Beautifully written—Kevin took me on an emotional journey throughout this heartwarming book. An enjoyable and uplifting story!"
—*Patricia Allen, Principal, St. Joseph's Catholic School*

"The book is remarkable, sensitive, funny, and caring. It is important for kids to be reminded that they indeed make a difference. Too often, they believe they do not really matter. This book will encourage them to see that small acts of kindness can change the world, even if it is one person at a time. This book is a real treasure."
—*Mary H., Social Studies Teacher, Minnesota*

"I started reading your book last night and had a hard time putting it down. It is very well done."
—*Darlene P., Publishing House Representative, Indiana*

"Just wanted to let you know that I finished your book. If it is any indication what I thought about it, I will tell you that it made me cry! What a great story!" —*Kathleen F., University Professor, Georgia*

"I completed *The Christmas Letter* in a day—that's how much I enjoyed it." —*Jennifer L., Housewife, Georgia*

"Rarely do I find a book that draws a tear to my eye. You have quite a talent." —*Jasen B., Airline Pilot, Colorado*

"I could tell that these words come from your heart."
—*Leonardo Defilippis, President, Saint Luke Productions and Luke Films*

"I finished your book, with laughter and tears. It is a gem of a story."
—*Marilou L., Housewife, Texas*

"I loved your book, *The Christmas Letter*. It was a really good book. I absolutely love the details, characters, and the way you thought up the story." —*Clare T., Elementary School Student, Georgia*

The Christmas LETTER

A Novel

Kevin Prochaska

The Christmas Letter
by Kevin Prochaska
Copyright ©2006 Kevin Prochaska

ISBN 1-58169-204-8
For Worldwide Distribution
Printed in the U.S.A.

Evergreen Press
P.O. Box 191540 • Mobile, AL 36619

Dedication

To Thomas and Marie
and all the good times

Chapter 1

It was the same dream that crept into her sleep, as it had many times before.

A gangly right hand appeared from nowhere, hanging in still air, surrounded by a backdrop of pure white. The dream unfolded as if she were riding on the saddle of the wrist, the hand moving forward with intent. Smooth, creamy skin folded around the back of the hand, the smoothness terminating against the rough ridges of knuckles. Beyond the knuckles, fingers curled into the palm, with the exception of the forefinger, which extended straight and rigid, pointing into the whiteness. The hand moved beneath her, the gentle pony, and she held fast.

The fingertip pressed forward to a weathered brass doorbell that came into view. Wooden steps appeared below the doorbell and a door grew from the top step. It was her door.

A bird chirped loudly. The chirp might have come from the world she knew now, or from her world then, but wherever the source, the sound chased away the hand and blurred the dream.

She stirred. The stillness slowly returned, and the hand approached the doorbell once more. The finger pressed the buzzer, long and hard, and a harsh ringing filled her ears. The ringing grew louder, drowning out a single, shrill squawk seeking audience in the background. The ringing stopped abruptly and the finger retreated from the doorbell.

The door inched inward and a girl appeared through the crack, an expectant look filling her face long before the ringing of the bell. The woman's younger self wore a long blue dress. It had been her favorite at the age of fifteen. The girl finally pulled the door wide open to search beyond the hand. Long brown hair surrounding her head glistened as she nodded toward the unknown.

The soft glow of a Christmas tree shone from the darkness behind her, illuminating her silver barrette.

The girl smiled at an unseen face as a white envelope appeared in the hand. As her younger self extended a shy hand to accept the letter, the old woman's hand flinched on the pillow. She too, sought acceptance. The letter clutched firmly by the hand crinkled as it moved closer to the girl. She smiled, as did the dreamer, both sensing some inner peace in its message.

The dream visited the woman often, and over the years she had surrendered all her smiles to the unknown messenger possessing the hand. Always the dream ended after the envelope turned to a snowy dove. The dove fled toward the sky as the hand opened, upturned palm empty. She could only watch helplessly as the dove shrank to a speck of light high above her. She'd awaken, calling it back.

But the hand kept coming this time. No wings grew to steal the letter into the heavens. The girl reached out, bending forward over the threshold, the door opening to reveal the full splendor of the Christmas tree behind her. The hand obliged, slipping loose as youthful fingers grasped the middle of the envelope. The hand retracted from the dream, and she felt a heart-pounding joy that echoed far beyond her slumber. She grasped the letter gingerly, sensing joy enclosed within. A lingering warmth from the messenger's hand extended life to the paper.

The life moved in her hand. She looked down, fearful of finding a snowy bird about to flitter away. She grasped the prize tighter, but found her own hand enclosed in a second, familiar hand. The girl faded from her dream and stood before her, aging thirty years. The vision leaned over the bed, closing her hand over the dreamer's.

The old woman opened her eyes slowly. She squinted hard, and opened them once more. It was as if she were bending over the bed, watching herself.

"Mother, are you awake?"

With her thin, frail body looking as though it were being swallowed up by the mattress, the old woman shook off the remnants of the dream. In the afternoon light pouring through the window to her right, she recognized the face of her daughter, legs pressed against the bed as she stood over her. Anna could have been her twin when the old woman had been forty-five. At that age the old woman still had her beautiful brown hair and youthful face. But she'd been much lighter than Anna at that age, for she'd still lugged mail then, and would do so for twenty-three more years.

Jim stood next to Anna, a blank look on his face. Jim always seemed to be a little bit lost, uncomfortable around his aged mother-in-law. His world was younger and cluttered by technical language. Inflated by his prominence in the business world, he loomed unqualified to descend from that pedestal to recognize the old woman's grandness. Five years older than Anna, he looked older than his true self. He bore no physical attributes that would distinguish him as anything other than plain and boring, the old woman sometimes thought, just as she knew it was the same thing he felt about her. Over the years, as Jim's position in the company had advanced, his hairline had receded. Poetic justice, the old woman once thought as Anna bragged about yet another promotion. But Jim had been a good husband to her daughter, and in the old woman's eyes, that accomplishment demanded her respect. She looked up at Anna.

"Just resting," she answered. "Supper will be served in a bit."

Time passed differently in her universe. It ticked away as intervals of emptiness in between meals. In the home, they all measured time this way.

Jim raised his arm, producing some flowers hidden behind his back. The smile on his face seemed forced. But she knew that already.

"Here Grandma Martin. Something to liven up the place," he said, looking around.

The red roses brightened the drab room, their perfume fragrance overpowering a faint septic smell. Though she'd always railed against anyone opening her window because of pollen, flowers next to her bed never appeared to bother her.

The old woman pulled herself up, resting her back against the headboard. She pointed to the vanity.

"Get that vase out from under that sink," she said, looking toward Jim. "Should be a clear glass one sitting under there somewhere."

Jim found the vase lying on its side, buried beneath two rolls of toilet paper.

"Make sure you get lots of water on the stems, Jim," she said.

Jim raised his eyebrows toward Anna, but did as he'd been told. A stream of water shot into the vase with sounds like the hissing of a snake. Jim placed the rose stems into the slender glass holder. He looked toward the old woman, hesitating.

"Put them on the window sill for now," she said.

Jim walked to the window near the corner to her right, stirring microscopic pieces of dust as he set the flowers on the sill. The specks lifted into the air, catching the light, and floated delicately to the floor.

"Next time put more water in that vase," she said.

Jim reached for the vase, but she motioned for him away.

"I'll put more in tomorrow," she said. "They gotta have water or they won't last long. Ain't that right, daughter?"

Anna nodded in agreement. Jim rested one hand on the sill, looking through the window. His fingers drummed, raising more dust.

"Nice view, Grandma," he said. "But they ought to cut that bush back a little. Might let in a little more sun."

"Wouldn't do no good," she replied. "It'd just grow right back up."

"Those birds out there are sure enjoying that bush," Jim observed, pressing his face toward the glass. "Chirping away out there like they're in heaven."

Anna eased onto the bed, sitting uncomfortably, as if she were riding sidesaddle.

"How are you feeling these days, Mom?"

"Pretty good," the old woman replied. She paused for a moment, as if catching her breath.

4

"This old body can only feel so good. It ain't like the car's new anymore."

Jim smiled weakly as Anna squeezed her weathered hand.

"Well, you know how long those new-fangled cars last, Mom. Too many buttons and gadgets to be much use to anyone. Why would you want to be one of them, anyway? It's the old models—the ones that have weathered the storm—that are worth the most."

"One could hope," she answered.

Anna winked.

"After all, what's a few scratches on the paint amount to anyhow?"

"Are they treating you all right in here, Viola?" Jim asked. "I mean, do you need anything?"

"As best they can," the old woman replied. "Some days are good; some aren't so good."

"How's the food around here?" Jim asked, grinning down at her. "I hear nursing home food is pretty good."

She hated the words "nursing home." It was a retirement center.

"Some days it's pretty good. Some days it's not so good. Just like anywhere else."

She patted her stomach.

"I guess I can't complain. I'm putting on some weight."

"That's not all bad then, Mom," Anna replied. "You were getting pretty thin living by yourself. I'm glad to see you a little heavier."

"You'll have a little extra padding on you with winter coming, Viola," Jim joked.

"Have you made any new friends, Mom?" Anna asked. "I mean ones you can do things with?"

"A few," she replied. "We get together and watch television sometimes. Sometimes we play bingo, sometimes cards. Worked on a jigsaw puzzle in the rec room last week—four of us. Didn't get done. Halfway through, the top of the box came up amongst the missing, and we didn't have nothing to go by to finish it. Somebody's darn kid probably ran off with it."

"I'll look around for it before we leave," Anna assured her. "It's got to be around here somewhere."

"You needn't bother, girl. We put it away."

"Can we take you for a walk outside?" Jim offered. "It's a pretty day out there. The sun is shining, and the air is fresh."

"Not today," she said, placing her hand on her nose. "My sinuses, you know."

"Do you get outside much?" Anna asked.

"Enough," she replied.

"I'll talk to the nurse," Anna offered. "It would be good if they got you out into the sun a couple of times a week. Might help your skin color."

"Ain't interested in no tan," she shot back. "Not at my age."

"Now that we've moved back to town, we can see you more often," Jim said. "Except when I'm on the road."

"How's Jimmy?" the old woman asked.

"Jimmy's fine, Grandma," Anna replied. "He's starting at his new school today. But he wanted you to know he'll visit you soon. His school is just across the street, you know. He had orientation today or he'd have been here with us. Now that we're back in Minneapolis he'll get to see you a lot more often."

"He's twelve now," Jim said.

"Time sure flies by," Anna added. "I remember when he was just a baby."

A silence hung over the room. Anna looked toward Jim.

"Well, Mother, we'd better be going for now. Let you rest and get ready for supper."

Jim nodded.

"We'll stop by and see you soon, Grandma Martin."

She closed her eyes as they left, the sweet smell of the roses filling her senses with fragrances of springs long since forgotten. Her nostrils flared, drawing in the pleasure that brought renewal. The same smell had filled the hospital room when she visited Anna after the birth of little Jimmy.

Time sure flies by. Anna's comment came back to her as the seconds ticked from the wall clock, the slender hand advancing with an unwavering regularity. Life passes as a single heartbeat, clear and distinct—she knew that well. If her daughter thought that time passed quickly in her world, the old woman thought, perhaps they could trade universes for a day.

Chapter 2

She napped the following afternoon, her head resting on a pillow. Her white hair, thinned with age, sheltered a second layer, yellowed and limp like corn silk. Slender wisps scattered across her face, reaching out as if to hide her wrinkles. Weathered skin stretched taunt across her cheekbones and irregular blotches of brown age spots floated like islands on the surface of the skin, medals awarded for her earthly stay.

She thought she heard geese honking outside the window. Her head rose heavily from the pillow. There were many of them, and they were angry.

"Shut up," she mumbled, irritated by the noise.

The horns stopped abruptly, and silence enclosed her world once more. A glow appeared, her eyes growing heavy, the light shining forth from a brass plaque hanging on the far wall. The room blurred as darkness swept over her.

Her domain was small, just over one hundred square feet in area, including a tiny bathroom in the far left corner. The furniture was sparse and simple. Near the foot of the bed, a mirrored vanity and wardrobe stood side by side against the wall to her left. At the head end of the bed, a white wicker clothes hamper leaned against the same wall, and above it hung a calendar showing the month of June.

A lamp stood in the corner to her right, its beam focused on an antique rocking chair. Next to the rocking chair stood an aluminum walker and a wooden magazine rack holding Christian periodicals and a Bible. On a hook directly above the rocking chair hung a gray sweater, the colorful insignia of the United States Postal Service sewn on one shoulder.

To her right, next to the bed stood an antique table, a white lace doily protecting a surface covered with a variety of items. An empty letter holder containing half a dozen ballpoints jutting from a well sat nearest to the bed, and next to it sat a cream-colored telephone with inch-high digits readable from the hallway. A plaque entitled *Footprints in the Sand* stood in its small easel next to it. A red pincushion rested on a bundle of folded cloth, the extent of a crocheting project picked at when weary eyes could handle the strain. At the opposite end of the table a wooden picture frame held the photo of the man she'd worshiped for half a century. The picture, somewhat deceiving, showed the man sporting a thick beard he'd grown only for a short time during the town's centennial year. But it was his most handsome photo and the one she'd selected when told that the space in her new universe was to be limited. An antique metal truck, painted white, with "U.S. Mail" stenciled on the doors, sat parked near the photo. The cargo hold had no roof, but sprouted like a flower vase with red and white peppermint candies wrapped in clear, brittle plastic. The remaining candies from the sack were hidden in the wardrobe. She'd eaten none of the treats, and therefore never found the need to refill the cargo hold.

She'd rested in her rocker earlier, watching the weather channel. Rain in Seattle—big surprise. The weatherman always wore a comical-looking yellow fisherman's rain hat when he spoke about Seattle, and his antics made her chuckle. Dusty winds kicking through Oklahoma—some things never changed. She liked the weatherman. He always looked *at* her when he spoke, not *through* her. The nurse's aides looked to her health when they visited, but not at her eyes. They chattered on like squirrels as they took her blood pressure and distributed pills, not stopping for replies, even when asking a question. The old woman understood them, knowing that she was but one piece of mail in the sack. But to the aides, who performed this routine dozens of times every day, it was just part of the job and not due to lack of respect toward her. When they did pause for a response, most senior citizens remained silent, content to simply breathe in the sounds of younger voices rather than partake in tiring conversations.

After Anna and Jim left Viola's room the previous afternoon, they spoke to the facility's administrator about allowing Viola to sit outside in the sunlight for some fresh air and a change of scenery. The staff had tried on many occasions to coax Viola Martin from her room, they were told. The staff, too, felt she spent inordinate amounts of time in self-confinement. But their efforts to persuade her had always failed, and ultimately they had abandoned the idea, mainly because Viola always grew irritated when any such offer was made; and they wanted no part in aggravating her already delicate heart. Grandma Martin rarely left the room for anything other than meals. As far as they knew, staff members told Anna, no one had seen Viola Martin playing with a jigsaw puzzle in the past week—or ever. A secret known to only a few staffers on the graveyard shift was the old woman's habit of sneaking from her room late at night, her presence in the hallway betrayed by the creaking sounds of her metal walker. They'd wisely turn away, allowing her to enter the prayer chapel undetected. She'd return half an hour later, and a series of hand signals among the staff would ensure her unimpeded passage back down the hallway.

The absence of the honking horns allowed her to nap once more, and a few rays of the afternoon sun crossed the room, lighting the brass plaque below the TV. The words on the plaque read:

To Viola Martin
In appreciation for fifty years of dedicated
service to the United States Postal Service
Through rain, sleet, and snow,
you were always on the go

Two snow boots had been etched in the brass below the inscription, the lead boot in the midst of taking a step and the second braced against the ground at an angle. The plaque had been awarded at her retirement celebration, where she spoke of her love of carrying the mail over the many years. Her only regret, she told the small crowd on that day, was that Oliver had not lived to celebrate with her.

She stared at the plaque for a few moments and then dozed off, hoping the geese would not return. Oliver appeared in her dream, walking past her, his boots crunching through ice-crusted snow as he delivered the mail. The crunching grew louder as he moved through the haze, each step hard and deliberate. Ice coated his beard, dripping to form parallel ridges across his mustache. He wore a thick wool coat divided into large red squares by wide black stripes running horizontally and vertically throughout the cloth. A furry black hat kept his head warm, running lengthwise from his forehead back and strangely resembling the profile of a submarine surfaced on the ocean. The mailbag over Oliver's shoulder grew as he walked, its increasing bulk pressing his boots harder into the crusted snow. The crunching grew louder. Oliver turned abruptly and walked directly toward her, a soldier on the march. The loud crunching beneath his boots increased, finally waking her.

Her eyes opened to see a stack of empty candy wrappers scattered on the table, the sweet smell of peppermint chasing away the fragrance of the roses. She glanced at the wall clock. It was three-thirty.

"Hi Grandma," a youthful voice greeted her between hard crunches.

She looked to her right to find her grandson, red-lipped with stain, creaking away in her rocker, his mouth crammed full of peppermint candy lifted from the cargo hold of her mail truck. Jimmy had rearranged the chair to face the bed as he rocked, but to her he appeared more intent on eating all the candy in the little mail truck than concerned about her general well being. A happy-go-lucky kid with a big toothy smile, he was skinny, with wispy brown hair. He wore jeans and a blue T-shirt with a skateboarder frozen in mid-jump emblazoned on the front.

She looked back at the table, to the pile of candy wrappers.

"Who are you and what are you doing stealing my candy?" she demanded.

Her sweater hung above his head, fanned gently by the rocking motion. An old friend, it had been her skin for more years than she could remember and could probably traverse the mail route just as well without her.

The boy was one of the interlopers, but closed eyes hadn't kept him from the room, as they did with the older and wiser.

"It's me, Grandma," the boy replied excitedly. "You know—Jimmy."

She'd known exactly who he was the moment her eyes opened. But he didn't need to know that.

"You were asleep, Grandma," Jimmy explained. "And I didn't want to wake you."

She grew irritated at the boy, for the items contained within the small room were the few possessions she had left. And the cargo hold full of candy had been one of them.

"Well, you did wake me with that awful crunching. And you ate half my candy as well, you little thief."

"Oh, Grandma," he shot back, grinning. "You kill me. You know as well as me that candy's been sitting in that truck for a long time, and you haven't touched it. And it's gotten kinda messy anyhow."

He held up both hands, wiggling his fingers, the tips red with stain.

"See. Look at my fingers. They got all sticky trying to get that candy out of those old wrappers. That candy was melting inside the wrappers—it's been in there so long. It's about time someone ate it."

"Well," she huffed, "and just what am I going to do when I want a piece of candy?"

He grinned, opening his mouth wide to show his red tongue. Standing up, he bent over the bed, grabbed her shoulders and pulled his body down to hug her tightly.

"Oh, Grandma, it's so good to see you. I missed you so much while we were gone."

He pulled away from her, freeing his hands from her body. His face suddenly contorted with a look of guilt.

"Oops," he said, staring at her shoulders.

She looked where the boy was staring and discovered ten red dots on the white sleeves. The blouse had been spotlessly laundered two hours before.

"Now look what you've done," she gasped. "Did they teach you manners like that in Atlanta?"

"Atlanta?" he replied. "Heck, no, Grandma. They're too busy still battling the Civil War down there. Somebody needs to tell those boys that their little fight is over and done with. I'm just glad to be back in Minnesota and get on with more important things."

Her limited storage space allowed for only a few blouses. The blouse she wore, now littered with red fingerprints, had been her favorite, and so she looked down at it with dismay.

"Hey, the red spots really give it something," he said. "Kinda adds something to your outfit."

"This had better wash out, young man," she warned sternly.

"Oh, Grandma, you worry too much," he answered nonchalantly. "Mom washes stuff like this out of my clothes all the time. She buys a lot of bleach."

He looked through the window.

"Hey, you can see my school from here, Grandma. See. It's right there, over this bush. Ain't that great? Maybe you can watch me at recess sometime."

He stood on his tiptoes, peering through the glass.

"You know, if I cut this bush back a little, I'm sure you'd get a better view."

"You leave that bush alone, young man," she replied. "There are birds living in there. How'd you like it if someone came by with a saw and cut up your house?"

He seemed to ignore her question.

"Why don't you open this up?" he asked, looking away from the window toward her. "Get a little air and sunshine in here. You know it's kinda dismal looking in here."

"You never mind about my window or my air or my sunshine—or me, for that matter. I do just fine."

"But you wanna hear the birds, Grandma, don't you?"

"I can hear the birds just fine. And other things, too, some that I'd rather not hear. Like that loud honking I heard a while ago. I could have skipped hearing them."

"Yea." he replied. "Those guys were lame. I was just trying to ride across the street on my bike, and all of a sudden all these cars started honking at me—like I wasn't supposed to use the road but they were. Was the darnedest thing. Who'da thought that people would get so upset about crossing a street?"

"You caused all that honking? And woke me up?"

"They did the honking, Grandma, not me. I just wanted to cross the street."

"Well, did you ever think about using the crosswalk?"

"I would have, Grandma, but that would've taken me half a block out of my way." He raised his eyebrows, adding, "And I was awfully anxious to see you."

He moved toward the bed and bent down once more, carefully hugging her shoulders with clenched fists as he squeezed his body into hers. She smelled the freshness of his skin and felt the life in his youth. He pulled free and looked down at her. She saw an optimistic pinkness in his face, freckles scattered like beach sand across his cheeks and nose. His nose narrowed cutely upward, and his eyes danced with uncontrollable delight. It was hard to be angry with him.

"Gotta go, Grandma."

Jimmy walked to the door and turned to wave. He wiggled ten red fingertips at her.

"I'll come back tomorrow, Grandma," he grinned.

"Wash your darn hands first," she barked.

As he left the room she looked down at the red spots on her blouse. A faint grin spread from the left corner of her mouth, widening toward the right.

Chapter 3

Sure enough, Jimmy returned the next afternoon as she perched on the bed, grinning widely as he leaned against the open door. This time she'd heard only one car horn blaring to announce his approach.

"Hi Grandma!"

"Oh, you again," she snapped. "Aren't you the little pest who came in here bothering me yesterday?"

She barked at him out of habit, for those who came through her doorway usually brought discomfort with them. They had been there twice already today, probing and prodding and shoving handfuls of pills toward her, expecting her to down them with a thimble-sized cup of water. They meant well, and she was grateful for their care most of the time, but the whole process always felt somewhat mechanical to her, like caring for animals at the zoo.

The afternoon light pouring through the window shone upon her white hair, looking for all the world like a bright halo ringing her head, although she would laugh at the very idea of one. She'd never admit it, but Viola had been waiting most of the day, hoping for the boy's return. He raised his hand and held up a red clay pot from which sprung a tiny green plant.

"Look, Grandma, what I brought you. And it's gonna grow a flower out the top. If we can't get you to open the window and smell them outside, let's at least get something growing in here."

"You take an awful lot for granted, young man," she scolded. "Besides, I already got flowers."

She pointed to the roses his parents had brought several days before.

"And maybe I like my room just as it is."

"I don't think so," he replied, glancing around. "Who would?"

"You're an awful big cocky pup for a ten year old, you know that."

"I'm a twelve-year-old cocky pup, Grandma. Whatever that is."

She already knew how old he was, but wanted to keep him feeling just a little unimportant, for his own good.

"So what have you come to pester me about today? Running in front of cars boring you?"

"I just came to see my wonderful old grandmother," he replied with a dramatic flair, pressing a hand against his heart.

He studied the front of her blouse.

"Hey, you took my nice spots off. Too bad."

"I spent an hour scrubbing your darn mess off," she snapped back. "When I could have been doing something else."

He picked up the metal mail truck from the table with his free hand and bounced it up and down on his palm.

"Hey, nice toy, Grandma. Whatcha got this for? You're a little old to be playing with toys, aren't you?"

"You just put that back down," she scolded, "before you break it."

"Hey, it's a post office truck. V-r-room. V-r-room. That's cool. Did you used to drive one of these, Grandma?"

"When I was delivering mail, boy, we walked. And that's a fact. Didn't have no mail trucks back then. Lots of walking. Miles of walking I tell ya."

"Must have been real boring, walking all day, I mean."

"Well, it wasn't. How would a young pup like you know what it was like back then? Your mother wasn't even born when your grandfather and I started carrying the mail. And I walked when I had her inside me, right up until just before she came into the world. Let's see you do something like that, Mister Smarty."

"Hey," he exclaimed. "Maybe I'll be a mailman."

"You?" she asked, shocked. "You little runt, you wouldn't last an hour out there."

He looked out the window.

"Hey, Grandma, look at those birds out there. They're fighting around that bush. Look at them go."

"You gonna hold that plant all day, or you gonna set it down before you drop it all over my clean floor?"

The boy put the toy truck back on the table and looked around the room.

"Where can I put this, Grandma, so you can enjoy it?"

"Put that old weed on the window sill," she directed, "next to those beautiful roses your mother brought me when she visited—while you were out dilly dallying around."

"I was going to school," he corrected, "not dilly dallying. Sixth grade this year."

He set the plant down, looking into the cargo hold of the mail truck.

"Hey, wait a minute," he said. "I didn't eat all that candy. There was more than that in there when I left yesterday."

"Sure there was, you little pig," she replied. "Maybe it just evaporated—into your pocket somewhere."

"I'm not a thief, Grandma. I didn't take any of that candy with me."

"Maybe you just ate more than you thought you did, Jimmy," she chided. "An honest boy would just admit it."

The boy peered once more into the cargo hold. He rubbed his chin.

"Well, OK," he admitted begrudgingly. "Maybe I did eat more than I thought. But you were asleep an awfully long time, and I got real hungry. I'll bring you some more if you'd like."

"Don't like peppermint," she snapped. "Colors my teeth."

She showed her teeth and then froze, realizing her mistake.

"Hey, your teeth are colored, Grandma!" he exclaimed. "Red."

She recovered quickly.

"It's my medicine," she fibbed. "Lots of dye in it."

The explanation appeared to satisfy him.

"Hey, Grandma, why don't you tell me a story about when you were carrying the mail."

His request surprised her for no one had asked about that part of her life in quite some time.

"You really want to hear one, or you just running out of things to pester me about?"

"I really want to hear one."

The rocking chair faced the door and Jimmy turned it toward her. He pulled it a few inches closer to the bed and sat down. Leaning back, he rested his hands on his lap, twiddling his thumbs as he rocked.

"OK baby, I'm all ears."

She watched him for a moment, assessing the honesty of his face. The boy reminded her of Oliver in his younger days. But she wasn't too keen on having a twelve-year-old call her "baby."

"You're an impertinent little pup, aren't you?"

"Ooh, Grandma," he said, moving his hands to his cheeks, faking shock, "Does Mom know you swear like that?"

"Impertinent is not a swear word," she argued. "I don't swear. And I'm as honest as the day is long."

Except for that one little infraction, changing a number once. But that hadn't hurt a soul.

"I'm just gonna have to start carrying a dictionary then, Grandma, just to keep up with you. I didn't know you knew all those fancy words. Now how about that story?"

She paused before speaking, watching him rock.

"Do you have to bounce that chair back and forth like that?"

"Well, not really. But it is a rocking chair, after all, and it's kinda fun. Why?"

"You're making me seasick, that's why."

"How could I make you seasick, Grandma? You're not even on a boat."

"How would you know whether I'm on a boat or not? Now stop that rocking. You're upsetting my stomach."

He stopped in mid-rock, reluctantly. Satisfied she had his attention, she began her story.

"Well, Jimmy, you know that around Christmas time we'd do a

bunch of hauling on our mail routes. That was our busiest time of year—lots of mail. And I mean tons of it. And like I told you before, we walked it all up and down the streets in those days—long walks—didn't ride around like they do today. And Christmas meant packages—lots of them, too. Now, Jimmy, you know what a fruitcake is, don't you?"

"Yes, Grandma, I know. And I hate them. They got all that yucky red and green junk in them."

"Well don't feel alone, son. We mail carriers all hated them, too, but for a different reason. They were the worst—heavy to carry, and clumsy. And nobody really wanted to get them anyway. I think what happened is that there were just a few fruitcakes made, just about the time God finished making the earth. And that was all—just a few."

She pressed closer to his questioning face, lowering her voice.

"Now let me tell you a little secret. Nobody eats fruitcake. Convicts throw them through cell windows into the prison yard. Starving people feed them to the dogs—and the dogs bury them. Even though thousands of fruitcakes are stuck in the mail every year, weighing us mail carriers all down and taking up room in our pouches when we could've used the extra room, none of them cakes ever get eaten."

"And so?" Jimmy asked.

"Well, whoever gets these fruitcakes just shoves it in the freezer for a year and then they take it out and send it to somebody else—more that likely someone they don't especially like. I suspect some of those fruitcakes had been around the world a dozen times or so, breaking the backs of mail carriers on every continent, before they just fell apart from being handled so much."

She pressed a hand against the small of her back, her face wincing.

"Oh, Lord, they got heavy sometimes. Just downright back-breaking heavy."

She scanned his face, glancing toward the doorway, as if expecting someone to enter. She leaned toward him once more, whispering while cupping a hand around her mouth.

"Just between you and me, boy, I think that way out somewhere in Wyoming is a big hole in the ground. The hole is real dark and deep—but it used to be a lot deeper. I'll tell you why it's not so deep anymore as it was when the good Lord put it there. That's because it's the Pit of the Unused Fruitcake. That's right. People sneak those fruitcakes out in the middle of the night and drive to Wyoming in the dark. And if you happen to see them standing above that hole just before they let loose of that heavy old mess of fruit and glorified cement, you'd see a big old smile on their face. And that's a fact you can take to the bank with you."

She searched his eyes.

"You believe me when I tell you that, don't you, boy?"

He shrugged.

"Sure, Grandma. And I suppose when that pit is full of fruitcake, the world is gonna end, right?"

"See, you do understand."

"Sure, I do. Grandmothers don't lie."

"You're pretty smart for a nine year old."

"Thank you, Grandma. And I'm twelve."

She pointed to the plant on the sill.

"You gonna water that thing before you leave?"

"Sure, Grandma. But who's gonna water it after that?"

"You put it there. You water it."

"I guess that means you'll be wanting me to come by tomorrow to do just that."

"You put it there. You water it."

"OK, will do. Every day."

He stood up.

"Gotta go, Grandma. Mom says to be home by five."

"Tell your mother to come see me when she gets settled in."

"OK."

He picked up Oliver's photo from the table.

"Grandpa. I wish I could have met him, Grandma."

"I wish you could have too, boy. Would've seen what a real man looked like."

His eyes suddenly twinkled.

"Hey, I know!" he exclaimed, his face bursting. "I'll bring you a picture of me. You know, so you'll have one to look at when I'm not here."

"I don't have any place to put it," she shot back.

"Oh, we'll clear some of this stuff off," he said, pointing to the table. "I'll find a place. Anyway, you're probably tired of looking at some of this junk, anyhow."

She raised her arm, covering the table with her hand.

"None of this is junk, boy," she scolded.

He studied the table, frowning.

"Anyway," she continued, "I already know what you look like. Why would I need your mug staring at me all day? Something that scary might keep me awake all night." She shivered. "Might give me nightmares."

"Oh, come on, Grandma," he said. "Who are you kidding? Mom told me you said that I look a lot like her. And she looks a lot like you. So if I'm scary, then you must be scary, too. You must be a real goblin, right?"

"You don't look anything like me," she snorted. "Why, when I was a young girl the boys would trip all over themselves trying to ring my doorbell."

She heard the doorbell and thought of the dream. The hand approached the buzzer.

"Wouldn't doubt that," he said, winking. "But I'm still gonna bring you a picture."

"You just do that and see what happens."

"Got to go, Grandma."

Jimmy hugged her, the warmth of his body absorbing into hers. His body held such vibrancy that she longed to cling to him forever, to consume him, to partake of his youth. The boy hugged her until he felt her grasp loosen, and broke away. Turning to leave, he stopped at the doorway.

"Bye bye," he said, wiggling the fingers of his right hand, and pointing to the clean tips. Then he was gone.

21

A few minutes later she turned toward the bed and tugged at the corner of the pillow. Hidden beneath the massive fluff lay six empty candy wrappers, a peppermint smell wafting from them.

Chapter 4

She held a handkerchief wadded in her palm, occasionally covering her mouth to catch the phlegm. When she coughed it rose from her throat as gray jelly, and when the violent bouts of coughing came, the cloth saturated with phlegm immediately. She tried to keep it a secret, hacking only as loud as was necessary to expel the slimy gobs from her throat and rinsing the handkerchiefs in the vanity sink when no one was around. Some days she produced almost none at all; other days the phlegm welled up in an almost continuous stream. But every day some rose from the back of her throat, seeking outlet, and as the times passed, its volume increased in frequency and duration.

Her eyes fell upon soft, red bedroom slippers sitting on the floor next to the bed, toes pointing toward the rocker. When she woke each morning, she'd swing her legs over the mattress and probe the cool floor with her feet, searching for their comfort. Sometimes she'd be startled, for the slippers suddenly changed into the walking shoes in which she had trudged hundreds of miles delivering the mail. Whenever the shoes appeared, her feet would begin to throb.

She waited for him, watching the second hand work its way around the face of the clock. Around and around it swept, ticking off second after second. She held the handkerchief to her mouth once more and heard swishing on the hallway carpet. Her hand slipped beneath the pillow. When it emerged the handkerchief was no longer in her possession.

She felt his presence in the doorway, but kept her face down.

"Hi, Grandma."

She raised her eyes, her expression solemn. His face was beaming.

"You're back?"

"Just like I promised, Grandma. And look what I brought for you."

He walked to the bed and held out his hand to her.

"Here, take it. It's for you."

She accepted the picture from his hand. Wallet-sized, a simple frame enclosed the image. He beamed out at her, his face as love-able in two dimensions as it was in three. The photo would add a bright star to her universe. She grabbed the frame with a hand on each lower corner and eased the photo away from her body, scrunching her face.

"This is your best picture?" she complained, pulling her farther head back. "You paid money for this?"

"No, Mom did," he answered, surprised.

He bent over, examining the photo.

"Why, what's wrong with it?"

"Oh, nothing," she said. "If that's all those fancy photographers can do these days, then it'll have to do, I guess. Couldn't they have thrown a little paint on here to help you out a little? I mean, at least make you look a little more human?"

He snatched the picture from her hands and made a face.

"Here," he said cheerfully, "I'll put it here on the table. Right next to Grandpa's."

"How appropriate," she replied. "The man and the mouse, side by side."

"Why, was Grandpa a mouse?" he teased.

"You know what I mean, cocky pup. Pretty mouthy for a ten year old."

"Twelve," he corrected. "And I want to hear another story."

"Oh, you do, do you?"

"Yea, Grandma. What's your favorite memory? I want to know."

She pondered for a moment, answering somberly.

"I guess my favorite memory is the one I ain't had yet."

Her answer puzzled him, but he persisted.

"Come on, Grandma. Tell me a story. And I'm not leaving until I hear one."

"OK, since you're such a little snot, I'll tell you a story. It's very appropriate, because it's about little snots. Sit yourself down."

Jimmy turned the rocker around to face the bed and sat down.

"OK, Grandma, he grinned, grabbing the armrests firmly in each hand. "Got my listening chair on. And I won't even rock this time."

"Rock if it'll settle you down, you scoundrel," she answered.

She sat up, swinging her legs over the edge of the bed to face him.

"Some winters we didn't get much snow," she began. "But it seemed like the next year we'd make up for it because all hell would break loose from the sky. You see, Jimmy, God is pretty good at evening things out—you're gonna find that out eventually. And when the skies broke loose, it seemed like every sniveling rat-faced kid knew it was snowing. And they were all out to get themselves a mailman with a snowball. Seemed like it was a right of passage."

"Did they ever get you, Grandma?"

"Did they ever get me? Phh—more times than I can count, Grandson. Been hit on just about every part of the human body where a body can get hit. Sometimes those ruffians would come at me one at a time, and that was OK, 'cause I could toss a mean ball myself, even with a full pouch. But mostly they'd come after me in packs. We didn't wear those heavy winter coats just to keep warm mind you—that thick cloth was real good at easing the sting of a snowball. And Saturday's were the worst because school was out. Then kids would ambush us in packs, and we'd get hit by dozens of snowballs until we'd finally tell their parents. Once in awhile we'd have the pleasure of seeing a hide getting tanned in the front yard—a real feast for these eyes, I can tell you. Of course, those scoundrels would be right back at it again the following Saturday. There's just some sins that are worth the penance, I guess."

"Heck, Grandma, what's a few snowballs? Even I do that."

She opened her mouth, pointing to one of her front teeth.

25

"See this tooth? It ain't really mine. I had to have it replaced. Some snowball hit me in the mouth the day before Thanksgiving one year. Knocked it clean out, and it went down my throat. Hurt like the dickens, I tell you. And no turkey for me that year. No dressing. No pumpkin pie. Just a vanilla malt while the pain from the dentist chair went away. Just because some kid got lucky with a snowball."

"I wish I'd have been there, Grandma," Jimmy said, irritated. "I'd have got that guy. No one throws straighter than me with a snowball. I'd have knocked his teeth in from twenty yards for you."

"Sure you would," she answered. "Hells bells, from what I've seen of the cut of your cloth so far, you'd have been right beside that kid, chucking snow, and I'd have been ducking twice as many snowballs."

"I thought you said you didn't swear, Grandma. You just said 'Hell.'"

"Hell's not swearing," she defended. "I don't swear. And don't be telling anyone that I do. I'm a God-fearing creature of the Lord. See, looky down by your feet."

She pointed to the magazine rack.

"See that Bible. I read it every day. Bet you don't."

He hesitated.

"When am I gonna have time to read a Bible, Grandma? Do you know how much homework I have to do every night? They keep me real busy at school, and then just to have some laughs at my expense, they pile on homework to keep me busy at night."

"It's good for you. An idle mind is the devil's workshop, you know."

Jimmy glanced down at the Bible.

"That's what they keep telling me, Grandma. But I figure I got better things to do."

"Like what?"

"Oh, I don't know. Just stuff."

"Does your dad still have his job?"

"Sure, Grandma. You know he does."

"Does your mom still have hers?"

"Job?"

"Her job. Keeping the family."

"Yea, if you want to call it a job."

"Hers is an important job. You gotta eat and wear clean clothes, don't you?"

Her eyes burrowed into his.

"How about your job?"

"My job? My job? I don't have one."

"You don't? What about school?"

"School? School? I don't get paid to go to school, Grandma."

"You might not get paid, Grandson, but it's your job, whether you think it is or not. So do it well. You'll get paid for your work eventually—you'll see. Don't waste your youth, son, unless you're planning to die awfully young. You're gonna be old a lot longer than you're young—take it from me. And you're gonna have a lot of time to judge the actions of your youth while you're sitting in a rocking chair as an old man. If you don't want to be sitting there thinking what a fool you were as a youth, then don't be one. If you're gonna waste your youth, you might as well not even get out of that rocker—just stay in it."

She searched his face.

"Understand me, boy?"

His mother had warned him of times like these, when his grandmother would amble on. Most old people did this, she said.

"Yes, Grandmother. I understand."

"It's like this, boy. When you're young, you don't do nothing but tell yourself how smart you are and how stupid everyone else is. But when you're old, you don't do nothing but remember how stupid you were then, but how you managed to get past all that. That's sort of God's report card—His letting you know you did OK with your life while you're still here."

But, at times like these, she had instructed him, just agree with her.

"By the way," she added, pointing to her fake front tooth, "just to show you how things work out sometimes, his younger brother christened you when you were a baby."

Chapter 5

howard shouted, "Hey Jimmy!" He was standing on the playground, poised to throw a football. "How about us playing some catch?"

"Some other time maybe," Jimmy replied. "Gotta go see my grandmother. She's waiting for me."

"You been going there every day since school started," Howard complained. "Why do you do that? Ain't it kind of gross in there?"

A third boy joined them.

"Jimmy's got a sweetheart in there," Trevor teased, pointing to the building across the road. "I'll throw with you, Howard, while Jimmy goes off to be with his girlfriend."

"Grandmother," Jimmy corrected. "She's old and lonely and don't get any visitors except me."

"Better you than me," Howard said, shrugging.

Jimmy picked up his bike and walked it across the playground. The school's custodian had complained to Principal Berber about the trail the boy's bike tires were beginning to wear in the grass, and Jimmy had been summoned to the principal's office and asked to explain why he cut across the grass when there was a perfectly good sidewalk nearby. Jimmy answered that he wasn't heading in that direction but he was going to visit his grandmother every day after school. The principal, apparently pleased by his reply, instructed Jimmy that he could still cut across the playground, but to walk his bike. All parties appeared satisfied with the arrangement for now.

"You think he actually likes going over there?" Trevor moaned, cocking his arm back to pass as Jimmy walked away.

Jimmy walked cautiously, guiding the bike with one hand while carrying a brown paper sack in the other. When he reached the sidewalk paralleling the road, he stopped and mounted the bike, crossing the street behind a passing car.

Viola rubbed her shoulder, feeling the pulling weight of the mailbag. The pouch always hung from her right shoulder, and like her feet, her shoulder ached whenever she remembered those endless years of toil. When she stood up she favored her right side, the leaning apparent in the vanity mirror. Her weathered body reeled from the weight she bore for fifty years, and as her skeleton settled, her body tilted toward the mailbag. Over the past ten years her body had shrunk a full two inches. For a fleeting moment her reflection appeared to her as it had years before. Her body straightened, free of pain and wear. When past surrendered to present, she sagged forward again, as if a plug had been pulled and the air had been released from her body.

Behind her reflection she saw the bush outside the window. The bush, at present, was home to a family of birds who lived deep inside the foliage. A pair of wrens had built their nest high, where the central trunk broke into smaller radiating sprays of branches. Hidden among the leaves, the little eggs hatched, and the baby wrens grew during the spring and summer. In the early afternoon, when the sun warmed the west side of the bush, the birds played on the happy side of the wall that separated their world from hers. The wrens, dull-looking creatures, darted about nervously, expending their energy with no particular end in mind. In their excitement, their feathered bodies thumped against the glass as the birds lost track of direction.

As the seasons passed without Oliver, she had become like winter's bush, living barren in cold shadows yet longing for the warmth of the sun. The birds had flown away as the leaves fell, never to find their way back.

Every year the bush grew a few inches, blocking out a bit more sky. During the spring and summer the bush bloated to a lush green when the sun directed its rays to the west side, but day after day she found the blackness of its shadows facing her. In the fall the shadows were reborn to vibrant yellows, oranges, and reds as the bush prepared to shed its cloak for winter; and during those winter nights, the naked branches became like skeleton's fingers, clawing at the window. The bush frightened her during this time of cold, for the wind brushed evil against the darkness, and the fingers scratched at the glass, seeking entrance. But the scratching of the branches warned of another intruder she knew would come one day. It was not his arrival that frightened her; he was no stranger, but the thought that he might deny her the dignity of acceptance on her terms did. In those uncertain hours, the pages of the Bible proved to be her guardian, and from them poured a strength. They had consoled her always, even when she banished them to the depths of a closet after Oliver's death. The book waited patiently in the darkness during the lonely and bitter times when the wrath of her sorrow turned to hatred of her God. But the closet door had opened one morning, three months following her husband's funeral, to the dawn of a new day.

She turned from the washbasin and eased toward the rocker. As she sat down she noticed Anna's rose blossoms on the floor below the windowsill. Flowers died quickly. Jimmy's plant wilted after five days, even though the boy watered it faithfully every afternoon. Nothing seemed to last long in the universe—except her. The clock on the wall boomed out like the timer on a bomb. She reached for the TV remote, staring at the second hand. The remote dropped silently to the mattress.

Time. Tick. Tick. Tick.

She watched the slender second hand move around the face of the clock. The shaft jerked with each tick and abruptly froze. The hand moved again—ticking and freezing—again and again over the course of the day. Each second performed its own ballet, unique in brevity, yet identical to the one before and after. Each second represented an instantaneous eternity, bounded by ticks, imprisoning the finite between. A nurse's aide checking her blood pressure once asked if she needed anything. Time, she told her. Bring me time. The aide must have wondered why someone who seemed as old as time would want more.

31

"Hey, Grandma, it's me."

Her eyes tore from the clock to find Jimmy leaning against the doorway, one arm hidden behind his back.

"Whatcha doing, Grandma, daydreaming again?"

"Never mind what I'm doing, boy," she snapped. "What's that hiding behind your back?"

"I don't know, Grandma. What do you think it is?"

"If you have to hide it, it's something you shouldn't be having. Or it's something you're ashamed to have."

"Maybe you're right," he answered.

His eyes twinkled, just like Oliver's used to when he was up to something.

"Well, you gonna show me what it is?" she demanded.

"Do you wanna know?"

He was trying to stir her up. She could see that.

"Well, sonny, if you gotta show someone the fruits of your sins, it might as well be me."

"OK," he replied, grinning, "since you asked."

Jimmy straightened up and pulled his arm from behind his back. He held a flimsy-looking mass of wooden pieces in his hand. Bent nails held the wood together.

"See, Grandma. Whatcha think?"

He'd built it himself and was quite proud of his accomplishment. Pieces of castoff lumber succumbed to his amateurish carpentry as he sawed in the dim light of his father's garage. His first two attempts were disastrous, and he'd tossed them into the trashcan. The object he now held was his finished product. He'd constructed a shallow box from plywood and thin strips of lath, attaching a wire by which to hang the contraption.

"Why, Jimmy," she said, "I believe that's the most unusual looking plant holder I've ever seen in my life."

"It's not a plant holder, Grandma," he corrected. "It's a birdfeeder."

Sometimes he couldn't tell if his grandmother was confused or just teasing him. It was quite obvious to him what he'd built.

"Really? A birdfeeder? Where did you buy that thing?"

"I didn't buy it," he said proudly, "I made it."

"You gonna hang it up in front of your house, I suppose?"

He looked puzzled.

"Why, no Grandma. It's for you."

"I don't know what you're thinking, son. There are no birds in my room. Look around."

He grinned.

"No, Grandma. It's not for the room. I thought I'd hang it outside your window—you know—to make the birds happy."

He pointed to the overhang above the window.

"I'm gonna hang it below the roof so you can see the birds."

Her outrage was instant.

"You'll do no such thing, boy."

The birdfeeder swayed back and forth as he stood before her, shocked.

"But Grandma. The birds will leave the bush and fly up to the feeder. Then you can watch them."

"The birds will stay in the bush, sonny. That's where they've always been and always will be."

Her words confused the boy.

"But you can't see them."

"I don't need to see them, boy. I just need to know they're out there. You know, you shouldn't meddle with things unless you're asked."

The boy thought back to when the idea had popped into his head. He thought about all the work he had done, and the hours he'd spent building the birdfeeder. He could have been out playing with his friends, like they wanted him to be. He saw no reason for her to be angry.

"But I made it for you, Grandma."

"You should have asked me first, Jimmy," she answered harshly.

The boy had done the same thing with the peppermint candy,

she reminded herself. Though he'd meant no harm in either case, he'd stepped across the boundaries of her universe.

"Does that mean you don't want it?"

She sat, thinking.

"We'll see."

He looked past her, to where rose petals, turning black, covered the floor. He left a short time later, taking the birdfeeder with him. A nurse entered the room to check on her.

"Nice looking boy," she said, studying the photo on the table. "Is he your grandson?"

"Yes, he is," she said proudly. "And he's a fine looking boy."

"He certainly is."

"He comes to visit me every day."

"I know," the nurse replied. "I've seen him visiting you. It must be nice to have someone visit you so often."

Viola sat on the side of the bed two days later, her short legs dangling six inches above the floor. Her head was cocked to one side like a curious chicken. She balanced on the mattress, an arm braced against each side. The afternoon was chilly; she could tell the autumn days were growing cooler. Her old friend, the gray postal sweater, hung from her shoulders, the empty sleeves touching the bedspread. The sweater had not deserted her, as the boy had—for he had failed to visit the day after the incident with the birdfeeder. She turned her head to the window and caught the brief blur of two wrens rising over the bush and diving back into the falling leaves.

So what if he didn't come? No one else came, either. Let no one come then, and be done with it.

The boy thought about what she'd told him. His grandmother had been right, he'd concluded, and it dawned on him what he must do.

"Hi, Grandma," he said, his voice more seeking forgiveness than offering greeting.

She swiveled her head away from the window, surprised by his presence. The insignia on her sleeve offered encouragement.

"Can I come in?" he asked timidly.

"Of course you can, boy," she snapped.

Beneath the gruffness, she was grateful for his return.

He entered the room, his left hand hidden.

"Got another sin you're hiding?" she snorted.

"No, Grandma. Got something better than a sin."

He pulled the object from behind his back.

"See."

It was a small, oval-shaped basket, four inches in length across the long axis. A handle connected the two long sides of the blue wicker, and the boy had poked thin pins through some of the openings in the weave.

"Sorry I couldn't give you the other birdfeeder, Grandma," he explained, "as much as I know you liked it. But my mom really wanted it."

He turned the basket in his hand, pointing.

"But, see here, Grandma," he said cheerfully. "In honor of you."

The boy had painstakingly stenciled the insignia of the United States Postal Service on one side of the basket, his unsteady hand painting a more abstract eagle's head than intended, but easily recognizable because of the bright colors he'd selected.

He pulled a plastic bag from his pocket.

"And see, Grandma. I got bird seed, too."

He desperately wanted to please her, she could see.

"What do you intend to do with that thing?"

"Why Grandma, I'm gonna hang it over that bush—if you'll let me. That way I won't be bothering their home. But I'll be feeding them. And we can watch them under the overhang. You can't hardly see them now because they hide in the bush all day."

"You're gonna scare them away if you go out there."

"No, I won't. They'll come back for the seed—you'll see. They did when I hung mom's up on our porch."

"Who's gonna fill that thing when it's empty?" she asked.

35

"I will," he replied anxiously. "Every day if I have to. I promise."

She mulled his answer. It was, after all, the postal eagle on the bird feeder that made all the difference.

The boy searched for half an hour for help to hang the bird-feeder. After some creative pleading he procured a stepladder, and with the help of the custodian, hung the tiny basket below the overhang, making sure the eagle head faced the window so his grandmother could see it. Jimmy poured seed into the basket and returned to the room, watching for the wrens, for they had flown away when he had approached the bush. Faint rushes of afternoon breeze swung the basket back and forth, but the wrens failed to reappear. Jimmy left for the day, assuring his grandmother that the wrens would be back.

The dream returned that night. A young girl once more, she opened the door to greet the hand, the Christmas tree glowing behind her. The hand reached out, offering the letter. Her thin fingers clutched a corner of the pillow as the white paper extended toward her. The envelope flew, a snowy bird disappearing upward.

She awoke to excited chirping, and rose, fearful of spooking them. Her universe dark, the birds were unaware of her presence. She approached the window, peering through a gaunt reflection to the birds greedily feeding three feet from her face. Her mouth turned upward in a grin as she studied the dishevelment of her hair in the glass. It formed a bird's nest itself.

The boy had been right. The wrens returned to the bush. The birds were more interesting to watch, she finally admitted to herself, than were their shadows. For the first time, she turned the rocker around to face the window and waited for the afternoon sun to warm the west side. The wrens flitted from the bush and lit upon the edge of the feeder. Heads darting nervously, they hooked fragile feet around the rim of the basket. Leaning forward into a sea of birdseed, they greedily consumed, their tails lifting to the sky. Cautious at first, they pecked only once or twice before flitting away, like mischievous children trying not to get caught. When retribution failed to materialize, they fed for longer periods, enjoying the feast while conversing in bird talk. A few sparrows attempting to dine were swiftly driven away.

"Whatcha doin' looking at those old birds out there, Grandma?" a voice behind her asked.

His hands grasped the backrest, her body swaying as he pushed the rocker back and forth.

"Whatcha trying to do, boy?" she scolded, turning, "shake these old bones apart?"

He moved to the side where she could see him.

"Hey, would you look at that?" he said, watching the birds feeding. "They love it. Told you they would."

He had arrived a few minutes earlier, standing behind her in silence, watching her watch the birds.

"You're just lucky they came back, young man. I was hoping I'd get to thump you, but they must have felt sorry for you. Even a bird has pity on dumber animals."

"I've come for my story," he declared. "Since I was right about the birds, I figure you owe me one."

"Since you managed to get so lucky, I'll do you one better than a story."

She pointed across the bed to her wardrobe.

"Go over there in that second drawer and pull out that book."

He did as instructed, finding a binder hidden beneath a colorful silk scarf. He brought the book to her, its dark leather cover thick and strong, and the smell was pleasant. A strip of leather across the pages held the book shut, and a lock on the main cover denied entrance to anyone but the holder of the key. She leaned toward the table, opening the diamond-scratched drawer. She reached in, pulling out a key and eyeglasses. She eased the glasses over her eyes.

"What's in there?" Jimmy asked anxiously, kneeling on the floor next to the rocker. "What's in the book, Grandma?"

She inserted the key and opened the cover.

Her most prized possession, her stamp collection, opened before them. For over fifty years, she'd collected every stamp issued by United States Post Office. Sometimes she brought only one or two, but sometimes, when she really liked a stamp, she brought dozens of them. Her collection even held stamps that the Post Office had opted not to release to the public. The boy's face, eyes widened at first by the prospect of treasure, now frowned as he realized the contents of the book.

"What's all this, Grandma? Stamps? Why would you lock up stamps? You can get all you want down at the Post Office. They sell them there."

"I worked for the Post Office for fifty years, boy. I oughta know they sell stamps. This is my collection."

"You collect stamps, Grandma?"

"Collected," she corrected. "I don't collect them anymore."

When Oliver died, she'd stopped collecting. Her man torn away, the focus of her life had forever changed. Only he had held the same consuming passion for the stamps as she had, and when he no longer shared the book's joys with her, it was relegated to the drawer. Viola had been a wise steward of them, however, storing them in clear plastic protectors like miniature photos, and each page could be removed by unsnapping the binder rings. A thin magnifying glass was stored in a pouch on the inside of the cover.

"There's a lot more to collecting stamps than just collecting stamps," she said. "They even have a fancy word for it. It's called phi-lat-e-ly, and a person who collects stamps is called a philate-list."

"Boy, those people must not have much to do. I mean, stamp collecting? Bo-o-ring."

She was offended by his comment, but continued.

"Maybe to you. But there are so many stamps out there no one can collect them all. There have been hundreds printed by the United States Postal Service over the years, and that's what I've collected. Every country issues its own stamps. And each country, like the United States, issues lots of different stamps each year. Every year they change the themes and color of the stamps.

Everything from moon shots to war heroes gets on a stamp eventually. Flowers to birds to old cars. Great events, great innovations, everything. And the cost of stamps changes over the years, just like everything else. A savvy stamp collector can narrow a stamp's age down real fast, just by the price on it."

She turned a few pages.

"You see," she said. "Row upon row of different types of stamps."

"What's that one?" Jimmy asked. "Say, I'll bet it's from another country—see, it says it only cost a penny."

"No, it's from here," she replied. "Back then, stamps only cost a penny."

She began to explain to him how stamps had steadily gone up in price over the years, and how they had changed in design and subject as the world had changed with the passing of time and marking of events. Even the way they were made had changed, she explained. As the boy listened, his initial disinterest evolved to curiosity, and then to a deepening appreciation as his grandmother described each stamp in amazing detail. She explained the pictures on the stamps, revealing to him major events happening in the world at that particular time in history. She knew why subjects had been selected and even why they were posed as they were.

"These must be pretty valuable," Jimmy said.

"The value of a stamp is in its flaw," she explained.

"What do you mean, Grandma?"

"It's a kinda funny thing about the human animal," she answered. "They find a flaw on their body, like a wart or a pimple, and right away they think they're somehow less attractive than they would be if that mark wasn't there. Or they feel if they add something, like makeup to their face or dye to their hair, it increases their value in the eyes of others. But the value of a stamp is enhanced by its imperfections, and oftentimes humans are drawn to something done more wrong than right."

She pointed.

"See here. Look at this stamp."

He studied the stamp.

"Now," she instructed. "Look at the one next to it."

He studied the second stamp, looking back to the first.

"It's the same stamp, Grandma," he said.

He thought of his mother's comment again, about old people getting confused easily.

She pulled the magnifying glass from the binder and handed it to him.

"Look closer, Jimmy. Look at them both."

He peered through the glass, passing the instrument back and forth between the two stamps.

"Hey, I see it now, Grandma. It looks like the one on the right has been smeared."

"You're right," she grinned. "The second one is what they call a double impression. This happens when a stamp is accidentally printed twice. Sometimes the whole stamp is double impressed, sometimes just part of the stamp is done. But collectors like this stuff. Some collectors concentrate just on certain flawed stamps, like double impressions. Besides all the good stamps out there, there's all the different types of flawed stamps—stuff like set offs, gutter snipes, and all sorts of other things gone wrong. They got lots of cute names for flaws on stamps."

"So the stamp gets its value from a bad printing press?"

"Actually a bad stamp can begin with a mistake in the design or a burp on the presses. Flaws come in two basic groups—freaks and errors. Freaks happen mostly during printing stage and are mostly machine made. Errors are design flaws—they're missing something that's supposed to be there, or some bit of information that's on the stamp is wrong. Errors are man-made."

"Man made?" Jimmy asked.

"Yes, boy who wonders why he goes to school. There have been spelling errors even on United States postal stamps. Sometimes they even get the facts wrong."

"Why don't they just throw them away then?"

"Too late, most times. They're already out there in circulation.

And sometimes the Post Office does a real stupid thing, like adding to the problem. They print more with the same flaw."

"What would they do that for?"

"Used to be, when the Post Office would discover an error, they'd flood the market with the same flawed stamp so it wouldn't become a collector's item. Back sometime in the sixties, I believe, there was a stamp issued called the Thatcher Ferry Bridge error. After this stamp came out, the Post Office printed up a bunch of them up to destroy the value of the original error. If there was a whole mess of them out there, was the rationale, the stamp would have no value."

"What happened then?"

"Some collector took them to court. Was a pretty big deal—a landmark case, because the courts ruled that the Post Office couldn't do that anymore."

She grinned, turning the page, and pointed to a rectangular stamp.

"And I got six of them buggers, right here."

His eyes followed her fingers, and he placed the magnifying glass over one of the stamps.

"Who's that man?"

"That's Dag Hammarskjold, and he was secretary-general to the United Nations at the time, or had been. See, it says so right here on the stamp. He died in a plane crash and this was a commemorative stamp. They print these stamps in steps, and in one step the bridge—the Thatcher Ferry Bridge—was inverted on the stamp."

She turned the page.

"Hey," Jimmy exclaimed, pointing to a dark-colored stamp, "look at that one. It's one of those old planes—you know, like the Red Baron flew."

"That's called a biplane," she replied "and I didn't collect that one. My dad gave it to me. He even sealed it so no one would damage it."

"And it's flying upside down," Jimmy said, tracing over the

plastic protecting the stamp. "It's doing a roll. I bet he's part of an air show."

"That's not exactly the way it was supposed to look," she explained. "The plane was supposed to be normal, but they printed it upside down. It was another one of those inverted pictures."

"Cool—I guess."

Jimmy pointed to an old touring car on another stamp.

"Hey, look at that old car. Must be a hundred years old."

"Well, not exactly. As you can see by the square body, it's a…"

She went on to explain all about the car—why it was selected to grace the stamp, why it was posed thus, and what event in history it signified. She knew the weight of the car, the engine size, the tire diameter, and the manufacturer. She told of flowers, birds, men, and events as the stamps marched across the pages. The knowledge flowed from her as she talked continually for two hours, sometimes appearing unaware of the boy's presence as a door to her past creaked open through the lessons of the stamps.

Perhaps Grandma Martin wasn't as addle-brained as his mother said, he thought as he watched her steady hands glide across the pages.

Over the next few weeks the boy and his grandmother consumed hours inside the book. Sometimes small fragments of paper stuck randomly on pages held scribbling about certain stamps. She knew the complete history of each—what famous person or deed was captured in the minute square of paper, who designed a particular stamp, and even why odd colors were picked. She explained in great detail about types of flaws and errors and how to recognize them.

"Grandma," the boy realized one day, "do you have any idea how much money this book is worth?"

"Money?" she replied. "No, Grandson, I don't. But I know what it's worth to me."

It was one of those things she said now and then that puzzled him. But he was content in his puzzlement.

When she moved to the home she'd received an offer to sell

the stamps, sight unseen, for a large sum of money. In her sorrow over Oliver's death, she'd been tempted to accept the money and give it to Anna, but ultimately had decided against it. It had been a wise decision. A greater wealth shone in the eyes of her grandson as he listened intently to the stories she told—a wealth not easily replaced by something as useless as money.

Chapter 6

Time passed quickly with the coming of the birds and the lessons of the stamps.

"Tonight's Halloween, Grandma," Jimmy said, his eyes dancing with mischief. "Boo-ooo-ooo-ahh."

He raised his hands, a scary face forming as he wiggled his fingers at her.

"If I come and visit you, are you gonna give me one of your peppermint candies?"

"Give you one?" she snorted. "Why, as I recall, you pretty darn near wiped out my stash the first time you came here. What makes you so sure I got any left?"

"Oh, you'll find some, I expect," he replied confidently. "After all, aren't you the crafty one who told me to enjoy my youth? Well, I'm gonna do just that by visiting you tonight."

"I'll be asleep," she argued. "Don't come 'cause I'll be sleeping."

"I'll wake you up."

"Don't you dare, you little snipe."

"What's the matter, Grandma? Don't you like Halloween?"

"Don't have time for Halloween. It's just for kids, anyway. Spooks and all the lot running around in the dark like fools."

Since the skeleton's fingers appeared to claw the glass, the seasonal approach of Halloween frightened her.

"I always liked Valentine's Day better," she continued. "It's meant for everyone. Candy and love mixed together—not candy and greed and goblins. Your grandfather and I loved Valentine's Day."

"Well, Grandma, Valentine's Day is about four months off. We'll just have to make do with Halloween."

"Well make do somewhere else. I ain't giving you nothing. You're just going out spooking people tonight anyway, aren't you, ya little heathen? Probably dressed up like the devil himself."

"OK, Grandma."

He stood up to leave.

"If that's what you want."

His answer disappointed her, but she said nothing further.

She waited until nine o'clock that evening, five peppermint candies warming in her hand, but the boy didn't come. Had she hurt his feelings? At ten-thirty she could no longer stay awake. She fell asleep beneath the warm covers of her bed, still clutching the candies. She slept uneasily, guilty.

A silent figure carrying a cloth bag entered her room at eleven. The figure worked swiftly in the darkness. The faint hallway light guided the movement as still eyes rested beneath bird-like eyelids. An aide passed by the doorway and stopped. Peeking in, she snickered.

She awoke early and thought of him. The five candies she'd held lay on the table next to her bed. Why hadn't he come? She stared at the ceiling, her eyes roving back and forth across the swirling patterns in the white tiles. She sniffed some familiar aroma and searched her memory for its origin. The smell was sweet, filling the air around her. Curious, she lifted her hand to re-move the blankets and felt small objects slide from her body and drop to the mattress. The objects clicked against each other like dice. Her fingers touched something tiny and hard. She picked it up and held it to her face. It was dark red and shaped like a heart. She sniffed it. It was candy.

Around her bed lay hundreds of tiny red cinnamon hearts. The candies covered the bed, so numerous they appeared to be part of the bedspread. Dispersed among them were dozens of larger candies, pink and red bumps, in the shape of hearts and flowers. A bright red banner, with painted letters her eyes couldn't read, hung below the clock.

Jimmy poked his head through the doorway, a big grin splashed across his face.

"Happy Valenteen's Day, Grandma!" he shouted as he entered, his hands raised, "Happy Valenteen's Day!"

"What's this silliness all about?" she demanded.

"Why, it's Valenteen's Day, Grandma," he explained, as if she should know. "And you just wouldn't believe how hard it is to find heart-shaped candy this time of year."

Jimmy placed his fingers on the bed, pushing up and down. The candies near his hand bounced into the air with the spring of the mattress. They fell back, clicking against each other.

"Found a place with a pot load of this stuff in their storeroom," he grinned.

"How did this get on my bed?"

"Oh, that. Well, you see, the Valenteen's Elf came last night. Snuck right in here while you were snoring up a storm and sprinkled all these goodies on your bed 'cause he heard you've been such a good little grandmother all year. Now ain't that sweet?"

As he spoke the words "good little grandmother" he pinched her face, pulling her cheek up and down. She brushed his hand away, suspicious.

"So someone came in my room, without my permission, and lied to you about me snoring, huh? Who would be so low down as to come into a defenseless old woman's room in the middle of the night and risk scaring her half to death if she woke up?"

"Defenseless?" Jimmy asked, looking around. "Did someone else move into this room since I was here last? 'Cause there was nothing defenseless about the last person that lived here."

He desperately wanted to know if she was pleased.

"Oh, come on, Grandma, just tell me that I made you happy. I won't tell anybody."

She imagined her grandson sneaking in during the night and planting a garden of candies on her mattress while she slept. She had to admit—it had been clever, and he had gone to a lot of trouble for her.

"I bet you just picked through your trick or treats and gave me what you didn't want," she said.

"People don't give hearts at Halloween, Grandma," he retorted. "And for your information, Miss Smarty, I didn't go trick-or-treating. I skipped it so I could Valenteen."

"OK, OK" she smiled. "I'm surprised. And happy. And by the way—Happy— what'd you say?—Valenteen's Day to you, Grandson."

The smell of cinnamon carried memories. This was just like something Oliver would have done. She wished he were here to share the moment with them. He would have been proud that Jimmy skipped trick-or-treating to search for heart-shaped candy just for the joy of pleasing her.

It had been a nice gesture—even she had to admit that. And very creative of him. She felt proud.

"But what are you doing here so early, anyway," she asked. "Aren't you supposed to be in school?"

"School?" he asked. "Grandma, it's Saturday. That's why I'm here so early."

She began picking up candies as if she were picking berries.

"And what am I supposed to do with all this? You know I don't eat candy."

He glanced to the five peppermint candies on the table, grinning mischievously.

"I know exactly what we can do with all of this."

For he had her day all planned out. That's why he'd come so early. He pulled the gray sweater from its hanging place above the rocker.

"Let's celebrate Valenteen's Day then—with everybody, Grandma. Let's give the candy away."

"Give it away?"

"Yea, give it away. Unless you've been lying to me, and you really eat this stuff. What else are you gonna do with all this?"

He was right, and she liked his idea. She would never eat all the candy, especially because she'd have to be sneaky about eating it.

"OK, then, take it. Give it to all your greedy little friends."

"No, that's not what we're going to do, Grandma."

"Gonna keep it all to yourself then? I might have guessed."

"Errrtt—wrong again, Grandma. We're gonna give it to all your friends."

"I don't have no friends," she protested. "They're all dead."

Death proves nothing, but confirms all. It was something she'd learned.

"You got lots of friends," he argued. "You just don't know it. Now get dressed and let's get rolling."

"Sometimes I think you're nuttier than I am," she replied. "People will be talking about Jimmy the Nut pretty soon. Mark my words."

"Let 'em talk, Grandma. Jimmy Paige and Grandma Martin— the Nuts of Friendship Retirement Home."

He held up her sweater like a matador's cloak.

"Now, what say we charge out of here and give them something to talk about?"

She soon found out what her grandson had in mind for her. Scooping up the candy, he helped her into the sweater and eased her toward the doorway. As she passed the banner below the clock, she read "Happy Valenteen's Day, Grandma!" printed in magic marker.

"What are we doing?" she demanded, as they entered the hallway.

Ignoring her question, he held her arm. Jimmy walked slowly up the hall with his grandmother in tow. The bag of candy dangled between them.

"Happy Valenteen's Day!" Jimmy greeted as they approached the front desk.

Two nurses and an aide watched them approach, their mouths gaping. The unexpected sight of Viola Martin separated from her room was something akin to birthing.

Jimmy reached into the bag and dropped a handful of candy on top of the desk.

"We're celebrating Valenteen's Day," he explained. "Ain't we, Grandma?"

She seemed bewildered, but reached into the bag and poured some candies next to his pile.

"Looks like we are, Grandson."

They visited many rooms that morning, dropping handfuls of candy on each bed or table while wishing each occupant a Happy Valenteen's Day. In some rooms bodies once proud and productive barely retained enough humanity to respond at all. In other rooms weak mouths mumbled incoherent gratitude upon finding visitors bearing sweets, the thanks of broken bodies more powerful than any words uttered. Some pawed the air like dogs, hoping the plea would call the visitors back, for even a wooden Indian improved the hollowness of a lonely room. They visited those whose youth was long gone, but renewed itself, childhood-like, once more.

She remembered their faces later, and fearing their fate, sent her God that night a petition for dignity.

For weeks following their visits, the two were the talk of the home. At the front desk the staff chuckled about how Old Lady Martin, wearing her nightgown and postal sweater, had roamed the hall passing out Valentine's Day candy the day after Halloween, sometimes to old folks who hadn't had a visitor for weeks. And they laughed about the old people walking around with red teeth and tongues from eating all that red candy, and how funny they looked. One night shift aide panicked upon seeing all the red mouths, thinking some sort of epidemic had swept through the retirement home. The befuddled woman was taken aside and calmed by an amused co-worker who explained the origin of all the red mouths.

But some spoke in hushed tones of how Viola Martin had finally lost her remaining marbles, at the same time conceding that, perhaps on some, a marbleless head could function quite creatively.

After Jimmy left that day, some would have been surprised to find out just how well Viola Martin still functioned. The diamond-scratched drawer slid forward and a frail hand opened, dropping a dozen red cinnamon hearts into the darkness.

Chapter 7

It was her suggestion.

"I gotta give a talk, in front of my whole class," he moaned a week later. "What a bummer. I hate giving talks."

"What about?" she asked.

"Famous Americans. It's for Mr. Tyler's history class."

Her reply was swift.

"Well, landsakes, boy, give it about something I been telling you about. What do you think I been talking to you about for the past two months?"

She grew excited and felt phlegm welling from deep in her throat. It began to tickle, so she swallowed hard, trying to wash the jelly back down. It worked, but her throat felt scratchy.

"I know that, Grandma," he shot back. "But what do you suppose I should tell them about?"

"Pull that book out," she said, pointing, "while I take care of something."

As Jimmy rose from the bed, she left the rocker, easing toward the bathroom. She knew through experience that swallowing too much phlegm would upset her stomach. Door closed, she forced the mass from her throat and spit the acrid blob into the bowl.

"I could use a drink of water," she said, emerging from the bathroom.

"Sure, Grandma."

Jimmy set the leather binder on the bed and filled a cup with water from the vanity faucet. He brought it to her and held it out to his grandmother, now seated once more in the rocker.

"This sure is an awful heavy cup," he said, offering it to her.

The gray cup with the USPS initials was clumsy and unbalanced, but it had been a gift from a dear friend, so she'd kept it.

Jimmy made sure she held it firmly and eased it to her lips, for the cup was heavy even when empty. She sipped, the water cooling her throat and washing away the remaining phlegm. When she'd drunk enough, Jimmy returned the cup to the vanity.

"Least I can take care of myself," she said.

Her prayers continued to be answered, for the home still deemed her well enough to remain on her own. She dreaded the day when they would come for her, telling her she was no longer fit to care for herself. She would be taken to that part of the home she feared the most.

"Now give me that book," she said, pointing.

Jimmy did as she'd requested, and turned to open the drawer of the small table. He found the key lying at the bottom of the drawer, surrounded by red cinnamon candies.

"Why, Grandma Martin, what have we got down here?"

"It's where I keep my key," she huffed.

He pulled a few candies from the drawer and held them up.

"Funny looking key, I'd say, Grandma. I thought you didn't eat candy."

"You darn fool," she defended. "I found them on the floor—on the other side of the bed. If you hadn't of made such a mess on my bed, I wouldn't have to get on my hands and knees to dig them from the floor."

A wren chirped loudly outside the window, as if chiding her for her fib. But as the human animal straddles the path of predictability, she did as well, too far into the lie to extract herself with dignity. Her grandson, sensing her uneasiness, however, did.

"Sorry, Grandma. I should have checked over there when we cleaned up. Now, tell me what stamp I should use for my talk."

"Well," she said, opening the book, "let's just take a look."

They perused page after page, until Viola spied a row of four similar stamps, each bearing a picture of a Revolutionary War soldier.

"How about this?" she asked. "They're famous, aren't they?"

His face turned skeptical.

"Famous, I suppose, Grandma. But we don't know their names."

She studied his face.

"Remember when we passed out that candy awhile back?"

His face grew puzzled.

"Did it make a difference to you that you didn't know the names of those people?"

"Well, no," he admitted.

"And we still gave them candy, didn't we?"

"Well, yes."

"Did those people know your name?"

"No."

"Well then, Grandson, tell me—what was more important, the name or the deed?"

He stood before his history class three days later, holding up the stamps she'd loaned him. He spoke with rising excitement, with a confidence of one who knew his facts, for his grandmother had drilled them into his head, forcing him to repeat them over and over again.

"These stamps were very popular when they were first issued, because they reminded people of the great heroes in our struggle for independence. Without these heroes, their names never to be known to us, we would not be the strong nation we are today. And in times of war, when our nation is in peril, peace-loving men such as these— perhaps even some of you—will rise, seeking justice—"

He spoke the next words slowly, pausing after each word as his voice rose, his finger poking holes in the air as he pointed toward his fellow students.

"—to ensure our liberties."

The room erupted with long applause, dying in a lone clap.

"Very good talk, Mr. Paige," Mr. Tyler said, clapping as he straddled his desk. "Informative and well delivered. And to the point. Good job."

Mr. Tyler turned his attention to the class.

"And Jimmy has reminded us of a very good lesson—that not

53

everybody who accomplishes great deeds always gets the rewards or recognition they deserve. We didn't know we could learn so much from something so simple as a postage stamp, did we, class?"

He turned.

"Where did you get your idea, Jimmy?"

A voice answered from the back room.

"From his girl friend," Howard shouted.

Jimmy's face reddened.

"Jimmy's got a girl friend," Trevor teased.

The class giggled as Mr. Tyler smiled, raising a hand.

"OK, class. That's enough."

"I do have a girl friend," Jimmy admitted, staring at Trevor, "Sort of, anyway. She's my grandmother, and she lives just across the street in the old people's home. She gave me these stamps to use. And she told me all about them and how they came to be. She knows lots of stuff."

"What does an old person know about anything?" a black-haired girl in the front row asked. "I mean, aren't they all, like, bonkers?"

"That's not so," Jimmy answered angrily.

"Jimmy's right, kids," Mr. Tyler agreed. "You all have grandmothers and grandfathers, don't you? How well do any of you know them? Have any of you ever bothered to ask them about things that happened during their lifetime? Or perhaps what they did for fun when they were your age? How it was back then? Well, have you?"

He scanned across a sea of blank faces.

"No? Well, it looks like your fellow classmate, Jimmy Paige, may be the smartest one of you all. Don't you kids realize that your grandparents are history—that they are walking history books, right under your very own noses? I can teach you the facts, sure—the times and places—in this history class, but they can tell you the real story. You want to find out about what really happened back then? Would you like to know the emotion of the times, the heartbeat of the country, the pace of life? We've studied lots of events in this class—World War II, the Great Depression—and sometimes I feel we just gloss over all these critical times in history because there's just so much you need to learn. You really want to know what was going on during all that? The best way is to ask the people who were there, living it. You want to know what's beneath the sugar coating in the book here? Or perhaps you're afraid to find out."

He waved the history book in the air.

"See this book? You can open the pages anytime and read it—the print will always be there. But your grandparents, sadly, aren't like this book. They're going to close one day and never open back up. That's just a fact of life. So ask them. "

He paused, looking around.

"For a bunch of kids who I thought were pretty tuned into things, you sure can miss the boat sometimes. And I guess we grownups do that just as well. People, don't miss out on the lessons your grandparents can teach just because you don't ask. They've already been through all you're going to go through and rougher times as well. And they came through just fine. That's why your lives are so much easier than they were for your grandparents. They made the sacrifices for you and paved the road for you—as you will for your kids. They have a lot to offer you. They've faced challenges many of you will never have to, many challenges you couldn't even imagine facing today. So I suggest we all appreciate them a little bit better."

He paused once more.

"And on that note, I've just come up with a little assignment for you, one that might bring about a better understanding and appreciation of your grandparents. Let's call it a lesson in learning. I want you to talk to one of your grandparents and get a story from them about some event in their life. I don't care what it is, just that it happened in the past and to them."

"My grandparents don't live here," Trevor piped triumphantly.

"Do they have a phone, Mr. Reynolds?" Mr. Tyler asked. "You know, one of those things that go ding-ding-ding?"

The boy heard his classmates chuckling around him.

"Yes," he conceded, embarrassed.

"Well, then you should have no problem completing your assignment, Mr. Reynolds."

He turned his attention back to the class.

"And that assignment will be due next Tuesday. That'll give you a week. I want three hundred words, typed or neatly written, about some story you got from an interview with your grandparents, or an older aunt or uncle, neighbor or family friend if you don't have any grandparents alive. You all get to be news reporters. I want to know what happened, when it happened, where it happened, and why it happened. I want to know how it changed their lives. I want to hear feelings. Not only do I want the story, people, but also the story behind the story. I want details, people. Details, details, details. And with that, you can go."

A slamming of books and shuffling of chair legs erupted as thirty students stampeded from the classroom.

"Nice going, Jimmy," Trevor moaned as they reached the doorway. "Just what I need. I haven't talked to my grandfather in forever."

Chapter 8

Three days later, Trevor was talking with Jimmy before school. "You're not going to believe this," Trevor said, holding up a paper for Jimmy to see, "but my grandfather fought beside Audie Murphy."

They stood in front of their lockers in the hallway of the school

"Audie Murphy?" Jimmy asked.

"Yea, stupid, you know the movie star who was a war hero. Made cowboy movies after that. Well, my grandpa was in his regiment in Europe during World War II. Grandpa said him and Audie were pinned down behind a bunch of rocks together for about an hour. Grandpa got the Purple Heart there—right in the rear end."

He drew close, whispering to his friend.

"Told me he got it in the heiny—from a Heinie."

Jimmy snickered as a black girl approached them.

"Get your history assignment done?" she asked slyly.

"Yes," Trevor said proudly. "Can't wait to turn it in. My grandpa was a war hero."

"Well," she said excitedly, "my grandma walked the walk."

"The walk?" Trevor asked.

"Yea, the walk. The walk over the Edmund Pettus Bridge. In Selma. With Martin Luther King."

As the week wore on, more stories emerged from classmates who'd thought their grandparents had nothing to offer. Students discovered an untapped treasure in these elderly people, many finding excuses for more visits after the assignment was completed. For the first time ever, Mr. Tyler, a notoriously hard-nosed grader, awarded every student in his history class an "A" for their work.

He posted the work along the hallway for the entire school to read. Almost every paper exceeded the three hundred-word requirement, a fact dutifully ignored by the amazed history teacher who was accustomed to reading sparsely written work thrown together the night before. Many students begged to read their reports to the class and Mr. Tyler granted their wish. Jimmy told the story of how his grandmother hauled the mail, hating the heavy fruitcakes at Christmas. One student told how his grandmother, trying to make lye soap, had invented a hand lotion whose formula was purchased by a drug company. As each student rose to offer a rich plum of untold history, proud voices swelled with "My grandfather did this..." or "My grandmother did that..." Each story was one of triumph in time of trial, some bit of the past their grandparent had revealed to them. Every child gained a better appreciation of their grandparents by finding out something they'd done. Trevor, who'd tried to dodge the assignment, ended up inviting his grandfather to class. Wearing his World War II infantry uniform, he told the students about chasing the Germans across France, while fighting side by side with Audie Murphy. The class compiled a small booklet, and every student took home a copy of "The Real Scoop—Stories of Our Grandparents."

Jimmy mounted his bike, glancing toward Principal Berber's window. The custodian who'd complained about Jimmy's unauthorized bicycling had sought work elsewhere, and Principal Berber, distracted by more pressing issues, forgot about the ban, freeing Jimmy to take his shortcut across the lawn. Jimmy straddled the bike on the rise overlooking the home, observing the narrow trail his tires wore in the grass. Nosing the front tire over the break in the slope, he plunged forward down the hill.

Quickly parking his bike, Jimmy skipped down to Viola's room.

"Got something for you, Grandma."

He lifted the plastic sack.

"And what would that be?" she asked.

She sat on the bed, watching the birds darting around the feeder.

"These," he answered.

Jimmy pulled a stack of paper cups from the sack.

"See. You can use these from now on, Grandma. That way you won't need to be using that heavy old cup anymore."

The cup on the vanity had always been clumsy and seemed to grow heavier each time she used it. Jimmy opened the plastic wrap and set the stack on the basin. He filled a cup with water and handed it to her.

"This should make things easier for you, Grandma."

She took a sip, surprised by the lightness of the drink.

"Why thank you, Jimmy."

He set the cup on the table when she'd finished and sat in the rocker.

"OK, Grandma, what's our story going to be about today?"

"Wel-l-l," she began slowly, hesitating.

"Well what?"

She eyed the cup on the table.

"Well, since we're talking about thirst."

She bent forward toward him.

"Can you keep a secret?" she whispered. "And I mean really keep it?"

He inched closer to her, whispering.

"You'd be surprised how many secrets I've already kept, Grandma."

"OK, then," she said, straightening back up. "Just so I'm sure."

She glanced toward the doorway.

"When I used to haul the mail in the winter, it got real cold out there some days. Just bone-chilling down right God-awful cold. You just can't imagine how cold it was, boy, spending hours outside like that. And if snow got inside of your boots and melted, things got even worse. Cold toes just ain't no good to a walking mail carrier. I remember a lot of times facing that cold north wind. It was a biting cold and left your face so stiff and red it felt like your skin was gonna burn right off. For a while Oliver's and my routes would cross about ten in the morning, and seeing him would just warm me up. Other times I wouldn't see him all day. And it got miserable out there."

"Couldn't you have carried a thermos full of coffee, Grandma? You know, to keep you warm that way?"

"Too much trouble. And besides, it was too bulky to carry with you, especially lugging all that mail. Almost like carrying an extra fruitcake. One carrier did lug around a thermos for a while, but it dripped into his pouch and he caught the dickens from people who got soggy stained mail. So the Post Office bosses said no more coffee, except on break."

"So what did you do, Grandma, to keep warm that is?"

She eyed the door once more.

"Well, son, you know I'm a God-fearing woman and all. But once in awhile, when I knew the weather was gonna be real cold out there, I took this little bitty flask and filled it with a drop or two of whiskey—"

"Grandma!"

"I was cold, boy, real cold. You can't imagine how cold I was. And I only had a swallow. So I carried this little flask around during the bad times. And when I thought I couldn't go on any-more, I'd do two things—I'd say a long prayer and take just a little nip. Oh, Lordy, a little nip of that stuff would warm anybody up. Of course, now and again, if it was really cold, I'm talking freezing hell cold, I'd say a little prayer and take a long nip— just to kinda even things out."

She snickered, her eyes dancing.

"But when I'd do that, I'd be blessed with two kinds of warmth—one good for the body and one good for the soul."

Jimmy shook his head.

"Grandma, Grandma, Grandma. Sorry, Grandma, but I'm afraid I'm gonna have to turn you in on this one."

He picked up the phone and pretended to punch the over-sized buttons.

"Heaven, yea, gimme God, will you? God, Jimmy here. Say, you wouldn't mind loaning me Grandpa Oliver for about an hour or so, would you, Lord? Yea. Just a little while. Why? Well, Grandma's being naughty down here on earth and I think Grandpa needs to come down here and whomp the heck out of her to straighten her out.

"You understand, God? Completely? Fine. When can he come down? Really? Right away? Thanks, God. I'll tell her."

He hung up the phone, shaking a finger at her.

"I warned you, Grandma. Grandpa's coming down. Now you're gonna get it good."

He stood up, walking to the door.

"I gotta get outta here before he comes. I don't want to be around to see what's gonna happen."

She picked up the empty paper cup from the table and threw it at him.

"Get out of here, you cocky pup."

Chapter 9

During his visit two days later, Jimmy asked, "Don't you ever get any mail, Grandma?"

His question came from out of the blue and stunned her.

"Mail?" she answered. "Good heavens, no. Who'd want to write to me? Most everybody I know who'd write me is gone."

"That's too bad, Grandma. But you sure must have seen lots of it in your line of work."

"You're right, son. Tons of it. And all I have to do is think about that heavy mail pouch and my back hurts."

A wren chirping outside reminded her of the bird from her dream—the snowy bird that flew from the letter.

"But I'm waiting for a letter," she blurted.

It was the first time she'd mentioned the dream to anyone. She didn't know why she'd blurted out the words, but the boy let it pass, and they went on to speak of other things.

He thought about what she'd said that night, noting the stack of mail waiting for the arrival of his father. His grandmother certainly had the time to read mail, and having worked for the post office all those years, she deserved to get some, was his thought. But how does one go about getting mail sent, he wondered, thumbing through one of his dad's trade magazines. An advertising postcard dropped out and he picked it up, scanning the words on the paper. He grinned mischievously as an idea formed.

Five days later Grandma Martin received a phone call.

"Hello," she muttered.

"Good morning," a voice greeted. "May I speak with Viola Martin, please?"

"This is she."

"Miss Martin, this is Sergeant Gary Walters from the United States Army Recruiting Center here in Minneapolis."

"I don't have any money to give to nobody."

"No, no, Miss Martin," the amused voice answered. "I'm afraid you don't understand. I'm not looking for any money. I'm with the United States Army. We received your postcard, and we'd like to have you come by and see what we have to offer you."

"What would the Army want to give me?"

"We have lots of opportunities for all types of people," the recruiter explained. "We have over two hundred career opportunities in the Army for anyone who wants to serve their country by becoming a member in the Armed Forces. I'm sure we could find some job you would like."

"Serve my country?" she asked. "Do you know how old I am?"

"No, Miss Martin, I don't. We don't ask that on the card."

"Well, I'm seventy-eight years old. Seventy-eight."

"How old?"

"I'm seventy-eight, sonny."

"Seventy-eight?"

She heard his chuckle at the other end.

"I'm afraid we've made a mistake," he explained.

"I'm sure you have."

"Sorry to have troubled you, Miss Martin. You take care now."

"Don't worry, sonny," she answered. "I will."

The recruiter hung up the phone, grinning as he picked the card from a stack and slid it into the open mouth of a wastepaper basket. He was still chuckling three cards later.

When Jimmy visited her the following day, she told him the story.

"You see, Grandma," he said cheerfully, "even the Army wants you. And you thought you weren't needed, you silly goose. I'll tell you what we'll do. I'll put you on my handlebars and we'll bike on over to boot camp. Whatcha gonna do—ride around in one of them big steel tanks all day? I can see it now—Grandma Martin riding into battle, guns blazing as the Mongol hordes flee before the wrath of her fury."

"Gonna do no such thing, silly. I walked for the Post Office for fifty years, so I figure I've done my time with the government. Enough is enough."

"But don't it make you kinda proud that they called you?"

"I guess."

He handed her a large brown envelope.

"By the way," he said. "This came for you. At the front desk."

"For me?"

The piece of mail surprised her, for she rarely received any, especially a large, important looking envelope such as this. She opened the envelope, pulling out the contents.

"Let me take that," Jimmy offered, taking the envelope.

The stamps on the corner of the envelope bore no postmark or cancellation, but that fact escaped her notice she was so curious about its contents.

"See," he said. "You said you were waiting for a letter. And you got one."

The contents of the envelope held an array of slick advertising for careers in the United States Army.

"See, Grandma. They really do want you. See, you can even be a chopper pilot if you want."

Over the next week she began to receive other mail, becoming sort of a celebrity in the home. It didn't matter that the subject was the purchase of aluminum siding, three-for-one pizza specials, or save the monkeys. To the boy, it just mattered that his grandmother got some mail. In response to all the cards he'd mailed in her name, she also received some phone calls, politely turning down requests from organ donors seeking healthy body parts and marketing firms pushing gels to soothe the many parts of the human body.

"I'm waiting for a letter," she told him again, for the dove had visited again.

Her words surprised him, for she was getting plenty of mail.

He'd seen to that. Two envelopes had arrived in the afternoon mail.

"A letter?" he asked, noting the mail she'd tossed in the wastebasket. "What letter?"

He'd come to her room for almost three months now and she'd grown to trust the boy. So she told him about the letter in her dream. His youthful face listened as she told of the hand with the pointing finger ringing her doorbell. And how she saw herself as a young girl, opening the door, the lights of a Christmas tree behind her, illuminating her silver barrette. She'd smile at the unseen visitor as the hand offered it to her. She told him how, whenever she reached for the letter, it turned into a white dove and flew into the sky, disappearing as a speck of light.

"What do you think your dream means, Grandma?"

"I don't know. Maybe it don't mean anything. I only know that I'm always a young girl in the dream, just a bit older than you. And it's always the same dream. And it always ends up the same way."

"Maybe it don't mean nothing at all, Grandma. People have funny dreams all the time. I know I do."

He changed the subject.

"But I got something for you. Something kinda fun."

He pulled a fat book from his pocket. She read the title— Songbirds of North America.

"I figured you could use something other than those noisy old wrens outside. So I got you something with real pretty birds in them."

He opened the book to a page he had marked, to the picture of a bird against a backdrop of flowers.

"Look at this bird," he pointed. "Pretty, ain't it?"

She studied the picture. The bird's brilliant plumage was a treat for her eyes, the radiant blue and reds shining from the page. Yellow blossoms blooming in the tree where the bird perched enhanced the beauty even more.

"It is. I wonder if it sings?"

"I'm glad you asked that. Let's see."

He left the room and returned, carrying a tiny CD player.

"Look what I got."

He held up a silver disk.

"You wouldn't believe how much trouble it is to get a songbird CD."

He winked.

"Almost as much trouble as getting cinnamon hearts on Valenteen's Day."

He popped the disk into the player he had brought and turned it on. The cheerful melodies filled the room as each songbird burst forth in song. A man's voice explained what kind of bird was singing and why it sounded as it did. As each bird sang, Jimmy turned the pages of the book, pointing to that particular species. He turned up the volume, and the sounds reverberated through the window.

"Hey, look!" he exclaimed, pointing.

The sounds of the singing birds carried through the glass to the happy side of the wall. Two wrens hovered, peering into the window like miniature peeping toms.

"Hey, what do you know," he laughed. "They think we're holding a birdy concert in here."

The birds treaded air but a short time. Their curiosity satisfied, the wrens flew up and lit on the feeder.

"I had a bird once," she said.

"You did, Grandma? Must have been real nice to have one."

"It was. A pet parakeet."

"What happened to it?"

"It died."

He placed his hands over hers, and the soft bird melodies continued.

"Aw, that's too bad, Grandma. How did it die?"

She was caught, embarrassed that she'd even mentioned the parakeet. It had risen like bubbles in her memory, awakened by singing of the birds, and she'd spoken more from reminiscence than to offer a story about the fate of her pet. It had been a blunder, she realized. Now she was forced to tell to him.

"Oh, come on, Grandma," he said, noting her hesitation. "Remember, no secrets between friends."

He was right, and she knew it. She began slowly, picking her words.

"Well, when I was young, oh, say ten or eleven, about your age, we had some neighbors who were moving away. The husband worked for the government and had to go overseas for a while. And they had this bird, a real pretty green and blue parakeet, and they couldn't take it with them. Now a bird was a kind of a rare thing to have back then. The lady of the house was real good friends with my mother, so when the family left town she gave the bird to my mom. Of course, my mom was excited to have a parakeet around the house, and I remember her keeping it in the parlor in this black wire cage hanging from a pole. We didn't have television back then, so we'd sit in the parlor at night and listen to this bird. He actually made a terrible racket, but it was music to these young ears, I tell you. One day, about two weeks before my mom's birthday, I decided to surprise her and take a picture of the bird and get it put into a frame. So I got two of my friends from next door to help me. We set the bird outside on the edge of this round birdbath and they held it while I went inside to get the camera. I tell you what, boy, friends are nice to have but you gotta watch them sometimes. One of my friends, think her name was Rose as I recollect, came up with the idea while I was in the house hunting for the camera, to pose her black cat next to the bird for the picture. About the time I hit the back door with the camera I saw the cat sitting on the rim of the birdbath, eyeing the parakeet. And the next thing I saw was the cat running across the grass with the bird in its mouth. That was the end of the photograph idea as well as the bird. I'd never before, or never again, saw my mom so mad as when she got home that night and found out her bird was the neighbor cat's dinner. Lordy, was she mad."

Jimmy laughed, his amusement rising as he envisioned the cat running across the grass with the parakeet, his grandmother in hot pursuit.

"Aw, don't feel too bad, Grandma," he said, patting her back. "You know what they say. A bird in the cat is worth two in the bush."

Chapter 10

She sat among her peers, looking around as she ate, the cafeteria a sea of elderly people. Crowded around an adequate table in an adequate room were small people growing smaller, shrinking, as she was. Everything diminished with age—her body, living space, and circle of friends. Everything. The food sometimes tasted good, but sometimes not so good. The taste often had little to do with the quality of the food, but how she felt. She'd slept reasonably well during the night, but woke early, exhausted. She was angry at being so tired, so lacking in energy that her body could scarcely move from the bed. The walk to the bathroom grew more distant, and she knew by watching the clock, was taking her longer and longer.

The lunch today was tasteless because she dwelt among peers, and they looked old to her. And she was one of them.

Jimmy came by early, just after lunch, and surprised her. The boy found the entrance to the room blocked by a stainless steel pushcart. The surface of the cart was covered with row upon row of little pill bottles, paper cups, and assorted medical items. His grandmother sat calmly in the rocker, a young nurse's aide bent over her, gently unwinding a blood pressure wrap from around her arm. Jimmy had never seen anyone in the room other than his grandmother, and the presence of the aide annoyed him. She had a pretty face surrounded by long sparkling blonde hair, and standing beside his grandmother, the aide looked even younger than her true age. She wore a cheerful blue frock with colorful geometric shapes dancing oddly on clumsy oversized feet. As the aide rolled up the armband, she rested a hand on the old woman's shoulder.

"Your blood pressure is fine, Viola," she explained gently. "A teeny bit high, but all in all, OK."

The aide spotted the boy, a football tucked in the crook of one arm. Slightly shorter, Jimmy felt uncomfortable standing across the rocker from her.

"Whatcha doing here so early?" his grandmother barked, more from surprise than anger.

"Got out of school early today, Grandma. Some sort of teacher's meeting, ya know. Even teachers like to play hooky now and then."

The aide left the room, picking up a bottle from the cart. She read the name on the label, and satisfied, emptied the contents into her hand. She returned, one hand closed and one holding a paper cup filled with water. Her fist opened to reveal half a dozen pills resting on her palm like eggs in a nest. The pills were various shapes, rounded tablets and elongate tubes, each with a distinctive color.

"Time for your medicine, Viola," she said.

Viola looked at Jimmy.

"They keep changing my medicine. Look at all those bottles out there."

"Now Viola," the aide corrected. "We haven't changed your medicine in months. You know that."

Jimmy watched his grandmother pick up the pills one by one and place them on her tongue. After each pill the aide would raise the cup to her lips, coaxing her to sip.

"You know, she can do that by herself," he complained. "She's not a baby."

"I'm sure she can," the aide agreed, as Viola took her final pill. "But I'm just here to make sure she does."

Jimmy watched the aide gather her things and leave the room. She didn't appear nearly as pretty now as when he'd first seen her. The aide wheeled the cart to the next door, searching her frock for her pencil. She pondered telling the boy that she was well aware his grandmother could take her pills on her own. What the boy didn't know was that old people sometimes took too many pills or didn't take them at all if they weren't properly supervised. And some elderly people, defiant in their helplessness, had been known to spit their doses out when no one was watching.

"You sure take a lot of pills, Grandma," he said, sitting on the edge of the bed.

"I get four meals a day here," she complained. "And one of them is just pills."

"What are all those pills for anyway?"

"Keeps my heart ticking. Keeps my blood pressure down. Keeps me moving."

"And I bet one of them is to keep you from chasing old men down the halls," he teased. "Hubba-hubba."

She reached out, punching him on the shoulder.

"Aw, I don't think you have to worry much about that, Grandson. I had one man and he's gone. And I ain't interested in no one else. I could never replace Oliver, not in a million years."

She looked at the football resting on his knee.

"Whatcha doing with that thing in here?"

"Nothing. Me and some of the guys were throwing it around. Why, would you like to have a quick game?"

"Are you out of your head, boy?"

"No, come on, Grandma. We could play right in here. We got room. But you're gonna have to slow down when you go out for a pass 'cause you run faster than I can throw."

He stood, cocking the ball back in his arm.

"Come on, Grandma, go long. Go long, Grandma."

He pumped his arm back and forth half a dozen times, his body facing the window. Each time he pumped, his arm moved in wider, more energized arcs. He reared back, set to throw.

"I can heave you the big one, Grandma. I can throw you the bomb. I can—"

He felt his foot slip as his arm swept across his chest, fighting to maintain his balance. The ball flew from his hand toward the window, and he felt his body fall forward toward the rocker in which his grandmother sat. The world collapsed beneath his legs as the ball slammed into the window. The sound of breaking glass exploded into the room, echoing into the hallway. Jimmy grabbed the rocker's edge, hunching over his grandmother as the barrage pelted the tile floor. Jagged pieces of glass shattered on the floor, bouncing up to fall back as smaller pieces. His grandmother's body stiffened to a corpse as the storm raged around them.

The noise subsided as abruptly as it began. Jimmy straightened from his crouch, startled by the volume of debris. The floor lay strewn with shards of glass and a large hole had been ripped in the screen. The football rocked back and forth among the glass.

"What happened?" he asked.

He spied an object among the shards of glass and reached down to pick it up. It was a pencil. The aide ran rushed into the room. He turned to face her.

"Is this yours?" he shouted angrily, shaking the pencil in her face.

"You could have killed me, Jimmy," he heard his grandmother say.

"The pencil," he tried to explain, turning from the aide to face her. "The pencil on the floor. I tripped on it."

"Look what you did," his grandmother said angrily. "Just look at what you did."

"You did this on purpose!" Jimmy shouted at the aide. "To get me in trouble."

"I did not!" she shouted back. "What has my pencil got to do with your carelessness with a football?"

His grandmother shivered in the rocker. He put his arms around her.

"I'm sorry, Grandma. It was an accident. I'll pay for the window. Don't you worry."

She seemed unaware of his apology.

"Get me my shawl," she said, pointing up to her sweater. "I'm cold."

Cool air flooded in through the open window. But fear made

her shiver, not the cold. Jimmy did as instructed, gingerly helping her don the sweater. With the comfort of her old friend now protecting her, the shivering ceased.

"Wait here," the aide commanded, boring into Jimmy eyes. "And don't do anything else stupid."

She left the room, returning with a dustpan and broom, and wearing cloth gloves.

"Get out of the way," she barked. "This glass is sharp."

Then she added sarcastically.

"Unlike you."

Humiliated, Jimmy watched helplessly as she picked up the larger pieces of glass. He'd shattered his grandmother's orderly world with his carelessness, and he knew it. He'd breached the wall of her universe, which opened to nothing she cared to possess, but contained all she held dear. The aide, sensing the boy's humiliation, finally asked him to hold the dustpan while she swept up the remaining bits of glass. Their eyes met over the dustpan, each silently acknowledging the other's right to be in the room, dampening hostilities between the two.

"I'll get the custodian," the aide said, leaving the room with the broken glass. "We need to get this window fixed quickly."

Alone with Jimmy, and relieved of her fear, his grandmother spoke, looking up at him.

"You know, grandson, you're no Johnny Unitas."

A jovial custodian entered the room, and over the course of the next half hour, teased Jimmy unmercifully about his potential football future, suggesting that the boy use his arm for more useful endeavors, such as flipping pizza crusts.

But the custodian could do little with the window that day except cover the shattered lower pane with a piece of cardboard. He taped a black plastic trash bag over the cardboard to keep out the cold air, adding to the darkness of the room. An hour later, the wrens, who'd fled at the sound of the broken glass, returned to the bush. The birds bitterly protested the presence of the strange cardboard, chirping vigorously.

The dream came that night, playing out over and over, each snowy dove fleeing toward the heavens.

When Jimmy visited the following afternoon, the custodian had just arrived with the new pane of glass. He removed the plastic and cardboard from the window. Both the glass and the torn screen would have to be replaced.

"You could wait in the lounge while I fix this window, Mrs. Martin," he offered. "It would be much warmer there."

"I'll be just fine right here," she assured him.

"Keep your throws under twenty yards, kid," the custodian teased as he left the room with the cardboard and plastic. "I can only get so much glass."

Jimmy made a face as the man disappeared, mimicking his words. His grandmother looked toward him.

"I'm real sorry about the window, Grandma. I really am."

She wore her sweater, for cool air poured unhindered into the room through the opening in the window. Jimmy looked at the birdfeeder.

"Looks like that janitor has put those poor birds on the run again. I'll bet they'll be glad when that window gets fixed."

"They won't be the only ones."

A small gray blur shot through the hole in the screen, startling them. The blur flew past her face, barely missing her nose.

"What's that?" Jimmy asked excitedly.

His eyes followed its path.

"Look, Grandma, a bird!"

The wren fluttered around the room, confused by the surroundings into which it had flown. It lit upon the table, studying Jimmy and his grandmother, but just as quickly flitted away. The bird flew around in circles, seeking escape.

"Get that thing outta here!" she cried, raising her hands to cover her hair, "He's gonna squirt on my head."

Jimmy waved his arms, cautiously at first, but more vigorously when the bird failed to move as he wished. He scooped his arms toward the window, hoping the motion would ease the bird toward the opening in the screen. Just when he thought he'd succeeded, the bird flew over him into the bathroom and back out, circling overhead.

"Hey!" he shouted. "I got an idea. Let me go get a broom and I can shush him out."

He headed for the door.

"Close that door," she warned, "or he'll get out in the hall."

Jimmy felt the door slam behind him as he raced down the hall toward the custodian's storage closet. Viola stood up, leaning against the walker, watching the bird. As it flew around the room it chirped crisply, the sounds magnified in the confined space of her universe. It had been years since she'd been this close to a bird, and it excited her as it hopped nervously from place to place. Her heart raced and she caught her excited reflection in the vanity mirror. The bird performed for her alone—she felt it—bringing its passion to her world; and her eyes twinkled with delight. Only she and the bird existed now, it seemed—in any world.

The bird lit upon the vanity and ceased its chirping. A second wren, attracted by the chirping, followed its mate through the torn screen. It also flew around the room, confused. Around and around it circled, searching, until the bird spotted his mate flying toward him. It dove hard, closing the distance between them.

She watched in horror as the bird smashed into the mirror, fooled by its own reflection. As its wafer-thin skull slammed against the glass, darkness fell upon the bird. Its limp body plummeted toward the washbasin, thudding on the cold stainless steel. The room grew silent. Pinholes of feathery eyes bore into her from its mate. Dazed, she approached the basin, peering over the edge of a bottomless pit. A grim reflection towering over the steel bowl first acknowledged—then accused—and a stilled body greeted her.

The wren stared up through slits, as if only pretending and would miraculously open his eyes and rise from the depths of the grave. She searched for life among the feathers. Her heart felt hollow, as it had when her fingers pressed against Oliver's wrist, searching for a pulse. A shrill chirp broke through the room, its tone one of confusion.

She thought of the snowy bird as she stared into the eyes of the dead wren. This was a warning—she felt it in the stillness. She heard a noise in the hallway. Jimmy was returning. She picked up the body, her fingers sensitive to the smooth feathers. She'd forgotten how soft feathers felt, like the fur of a kitten. She felt the warmth of its life. Her hand opened, the body tiny on her palm. The wrens always appeared larger outside the window, their wings opened, and their bodies fluttering about. But the warmth, more than softness or size, drew her now.

She heard the door handle turn. The boy had brought too much joy to witness this death, or partake of its consequence. She slipped the body into her sweater pocket but panicked at the bulge. It would attract attention, followed by discovery, and ultimately, condemnation. Hastily retrieving the body, she brushed aside the old friend and eased the bird into the pocket of her dress. She straightened the sweater, the secret hidden from sight. The door opened and Jimmy appeared, carrying a pad of white paper. The bird flew from the basin.

"I couldn't find a broom to shush him away," he explained, holding up the pad, "but I got this."

He looked around the room, spotting the circling bird.

"Gee, you think he'd be getting tired of all that flying."

Jimmy waved the pad.

"Here, birdy, birdy," he said, pointing to the torn screen. "Time to go now. Out. Go back to your own home."

The bird chirped as it flew, dodging the notepad. Jimmy waved the wren toward the window, where it shot through the hole to freedom.

"Whew," Jimmy said with relief, "lots of excitement here lately, Grandma."

The custodian arrived a few minutes later. Thirty minutes later he completed repairs on the window and left.

"Good as new, Grandma," Jimmy said. "You see, nothing hurt."

The bird grew cold against her thigh, the body stiffening. She fought the urge to shiver.

"It's chilly in here," she told him.

"The room will warm up now, Grandma," he assured her, smiling, "now that the glass is fixed. That November air won't be getting in here tonight."

He put his arm around her shoulder.

"But from now on, Grandma, I won't be bringing any more footballs with me. I promise."

Chapter 11

The sound of crushing bones haunted her after the death of the wren.

Immune to danger she eased along the sidewalk gorged with Christmas shoppers. Her path blocked, she stepped into the street, her youthful legs whisking her briskly along the fringe of the crowd. She had no warning; her back was turned as the delivery truck neared. The driver braced for impact as the ominous screech of tires against pavement filled the air. An unseen hand grabbed her shoulder, shoving her roughly back onto the sidewalk. But the cat ran into the street.

Although the incident occurred more than sixty years before, she still heard the crunching of the bones and witnessed sharp, frantic claws raking unfeeling rubber as the image of the crushed cat's eyes strained from their sockets like huge fleeing marbles continued to shock her. In the final microseconds of those nine lives, the eyes betrayed futility and died in that resignation.

When she'd finished shopping thirty minutes later, the cat still slumped near the curb, eyes bulging, staring at her in death. The bloody mass, pulpy now under the weight of many tires, interfered with the spirit of the season, and a city worker was summoned to remove the carcass from the street. The man picked the remains up by the tail and flung the body into the nearby river.

She wanted no repeat of that barbarous act for the wren. The end of its journey would be marked with dignity. And she would ensure the task was done.

She'd carried the cold body with her now for two days, hidden, putting a plan together in her mind. Sometimes, alone, she'd smooth her dress, patting the bulge flat to maintain the secret beneath the cloth, and assuring herself that the body was still in her care. For two nights she'd slept with the bird beneath her pillow. The feathered mass kept the body warm.

At lunch now, she gazed in the shallow bowl of her spoon, and through her inverted reflection the plan unfolded. But she'd have to do it alone. Jimmy couldn't help, for he was unaware of the fate of the wren, and needed to remain so. He didn't understand death yet, as it needed to be understood. He was immune, as she had been with the cat. She looked around the cafeteria, feeling guilty about the crime she was about to commit, but knowing it needed to be done, confident her Maker would forgive her for this deed. As her lunch mates engaged in idle conversation, she slipped the spoon over the edge of the table and eased it into her dress pocket. She waited until after Jimmy's afternoon visit to begin preparations. She sealed her universe with a closed door to keep out the interlopers. Kneeling before the wardrobe, she slid a drawer open, peeling away layers of clothing to expose a gold-colored silk scarf folded neatly on top the stamp binder. A small square of cedar wood resting on the scarf permeated the silk, the sweet fragrance rising into the air. Bold swirling patterns flowed throughout the fabric, and hundreds of slender golden threads formed fringe around the border. Oliver had given the scarf to her many years before, but she'd never worn it, telling him that the gift was so nice that she wanted it to stay nice. In actuality, the scarf was a bit too loud for her conservative tastes to be wearing in public. Oliver, gentle heart that he had been, had, unfortunately, never been much for fashion awareness.

She pressed the scarf against her nose and mouth like a handkerchief, breathing in the sweet scent of the cedar. Visions of her parlor chest, with all its treasures, floated in her mind. She pushed the scarf up to cover her eyes and found Oliver rocking contently in his favorite chair.

She pulled the scarf away and stood up, closing the drawer. Moving to the bed, she unfolded the cloth fully into a large square. She stretched it at the corners, smoothing out the wrinkles and pulling on the fringe until everything was straightened and flat.

Regretfully, the time had come. She remembered checking her hairpins before entering the church, following Oliver's coffin down the long aisle to the altar, and now found one hand patting the top of her head. The time had arrived once more to walk forward with the coffin. Beneath her rib cage, her heart fluttered like the wings of a butterfly.

The bird, stiff and cold, rose from her pocket, and she placed it gently on the scarf. The body floated on the calm, a mere speck on its own sea. She folded the upper left corner over the body and then the top right, and repeated the motion at the bottom corners. She picked the scarf up, rolling the sides toward the center as if making bread dough. That completed, she folded the excess cloth above the head and below the tail inward. The shroud was laid. The cedar fragrance stirred, rising to her nostrils with its sweetness. Satisfied with the tightness of the binding, she secured the fabric with a thin shank of white yarn. She placed the bundle into her dress pocket and patted the opposite pocket, feeling the spoon. She pulled her old friend, the postal sweater, from its hanger. They would make the delivery as one.

She was ready. The walker eased into the hallway, her walker squeaking with every step. She was aware that the staff knew of her nightly visits to the prayer chapel, their silent tolerance of breaking retirement home protocol granted as reward for endurance. Her cane, normally left in the corner behind her door, dangled from the edge of the walker.

She walked the hallway slowly, giving no hint of the unusual. Opening the chapel door, she glanced back toward the direction from which she'd come. The chapel door opened far wider than was necessary for entrance into the room and had been designed to close slowly, ensuring the elderly would be granted ample time to pass through. She'd thought of this as she'd made her plans that afternoon, chuckling how she would use this instrument of old age to fool the youth. No one would bother her as she prayed—she knew that. As the door creaked shut it shielded her movement, and she continued down the hallway at escapee pace, turning left at an intersecting corridor.

She heard the door close and listened for telltale footsteps, but heard none. At the end of the corridor stood an exit door, and she made her way toward it. She pressed the flat of her palm against a large red button left of the door and pushed firmly until the button illuminated. With the alarm temporarily deactivated, she had a window of time necessary to escape. Plucking the cane from a metal rung, she braced the rubber stopper against the floor and freed herself of the walker. She pushed open the door to the outside world, the night air cold and unfeeling. She hesitated for a moment, fearful, but stepped across the threshold, her cane probing the ground. The door closed silently behind her as the red button dimmed.

In the cool air, her thin skin shivered beneath the sweater. A chilling mist filled her lungs, her breath swirling as frosty clouds when she exhaled. In the distance, across the black ribbon of street, Jimmy's school loomed. The night sky was clear, each pin of light above twinkling, as if approving of her actions. The vastness frightened her at first—the millions of eyes watching—but she found her grit, and reminded herself of the importance of her mission. She looked to her left, to the rows of retirement home windows, each one a separate universe bound behind a frame of glass. She turned and began shuffling forward, the light from each window guiding her steps as she poked her cane in the grass. The walk proved strenuous, for the thick grass gave way beneath her slippers, slowing her progress, and a cold frost coating each blade crunched beneath her feet, the sound magnified in the silence of the night. She wondered what would happen if she fell, and how long she would have to lie on the cold ground before she was found. She stopped once to rest, continuing at a snail's pace. At last she found the marker.

She peeked over the top of the bush, making certain it was her room behind the glass. The hallway light cast shadows through the crack beneath her closed door, and she recognized the rocking chair through the glow. She was where she needed to be. Moving closer to the bush, she struggled to bend over, and knelt on the freezing dirt. It had been years since such a hungry cold had penetrated her body. It shivered through her legs, roving upward. Thousands of prickles popped from her arms and legs, protesting the cold. As her body heat warmed the ground beneath her knees, the prickles retreated beneath the shelter of her skin. Her sweater scraped the moist earth as she leaned toward the bush. A sharp pain stabbed at her chest—angry butterflies—but subsided, and she continued her work.

She pulled the spoon from her pocket, rubbing the silver bowl with her fingers. The bowl had to be clean; for it was bad luck to dig a grave with a dirty shovel. She plunged the rounded tip into the soil beneath the bush. The soil was surprisingly soft, the protective branches above it trapping moisture in the pores of the dirt. She dug clumsily, spooning out the dirt, building a small pile next to the hole. She stopped once, frightened that the dead wren's mate might be watching from the shadows. The stark skeleton's fingers that grew from the bush in the winter stretched toward her to avenge the dead bird, reaching out to entwine her neck—to seek justice for that portion of its life that was stolen by the death of the wren. Determined to go through with her plan she declared, "You are just a bush. And I will set this bird beneath you, your roots will nourish from him, and you will have him back once more within your branches."

The hole grew to a five-inch bowl. It was deep enough, she concluded, and stopped her digging. Her hand trembled as she removed the body from her dress pocket. She lifted the bundle to her face. Peeling back the top of the scarf, she exposed the little head to the night. She grew sad looking at the closed eyes.

"Good-bye, friend," she whispered, kissing the feathers on top the bird's head.

Those had been her final words to Oliver as the lid closed on his coffin, and they seemed appropriate right now. Silent, unfeeling eyes stared back at her through the darkness. A symphonic curtain opened for an instant, and infinite rows of colorful song-birds sang melodies from a forever tree. She had no music, but felt the burial would be unfulfilled without a song. Worn lips puckered and wetted against her tongue, and she fought to push the music from within. The first note came hard and sharp, reluctant to leave the safety of her lips, shivering coldly as it came. The low whistling sound pierced the air weakly, but from some nearby tree a bird answered. She stopped, listening to the chirp, her heart gladdened by the reply. A second note escaped and she whistled again, softly, giving back the song the bird had delivered countless times to her. Her notes weakened, the melody broken by gasps for air.

When she finished, she pulled the bundle to her lips and kissed the little head once more. She covered the bird's head and placed the body into a hole so dark her hand appeared to have been cut off at the wrist. She pulled away from the pit, her hand empty. She began to cover the hole with loose dirt, spooning the pile over the edge. She stopped midway through her work and placed a flat stone in the hole, then continued filling. She piled the dirt high, sprinkling leaves over the hump to hide the grave. No tombstone would mark the resting place.

She stood up, peering through her window. Her universe seemed remote as the stars consumed her.

She felt a hand on her shoulder.

"Viola," a kind voice asked, "is that you? What in the world are you doing out here this time of night?"

She hid the spoon in her pocket as she turned to face the aide. Absolution would come in the imitation of an old fogy. She knew that well.

"I-I-don't recall—coming out," she stammered.

"Well, let's get you back indoors, Viola, for heaven sakes. Don't be wandering out here in November. It's too cold."

They found her outside, looking in. The following morning they phoned Anna, informing her of her mother's infraction, as required. This might be the time to think about placing Grandma

Martin in the nursing home wing, they suggested. They could keep a keener eye on her there.

Their keener eyes weren't on her, however, when Viola snuck the cleaned spoon back into the cafeteria later that same day. She was, after all, not a thief.

Chapter 12

Jimmy teased the following afternoon, "So you were being a naughty grandma last night, were you? What were you trying to do, Grandma, break outta the joint?"

The boy had overheard the story when the administrator phoned his mother early that morning to inform her that Viola Martin had been found wandering outside the building after dark.

"No, you blamed fool," she retorted. "I just went outside to get some fresh air. Can't a body do anything without all this commotion? Then I was going to do some praying at the chapel for that heathen soul of yours."

She couldn't tell him, or anyone, the real reason why she'd ventured outside in the cold and darkness, to bury a dead bird; to bestow upon it some dignity at the end of its short life, a respect that hadn't been granted to the cat. They'd all think she was daft.

"Sure you were, Grandma," he replied sarcastically. "I bet you were heading for a hot poker game somewhere. Look at those wet slippers."

The slippers sat on the floor next to the bed where she'd left them to dry. She had been forced to wear leather flats all day and their confining interior made her feet throb. Jimmy picked up the wet slippers.

"Why don't I put these over the hot air duct so they'll dry out."

Just inside the hallway door a heat duct covered a small rectangle of the floor. Jimmy set the slippers upside down over the metal cover, feeling hot air rising to warm the footwear.

"This'll dry them right out, Grandma."

She moved in the rocker, wincing in pain.

"What's the matter, Grandma?"

"It's these darn shoes. Ain't used to them, and they're pinching my feet."

"Here, let me take them off for you," he offered.

She wanted to protest, but before she could, he knelt before her, gingerly lifting her right foot to remove the shoe. The tight leather had dug a deep impression where the shoe had pressed against her skin all day. With the shoe off, her foot felt immediate relief, and she wiggled her toes to restore the blood circulation. He pulled off the remaining shoe, studying her feet.

"Hey, I know!" he yelled excitedly, "let's soak your feet, Grandma. That'll make them feel real good."

Before she could reply he rushed off down the hallway, searching for a pan. Her feet ached badly, and a good soaking would be wonderful. A few minutes later Jimmy returned, a white roasting pan in hand.

"Borrowed it from the kitchen," he said proudly.

"Lord Almighty, Jimmy. I thought we were gonna soak 'em, not roast 'em."

"Look at what else I got."

He held up a blue bottle. Where he had gotten that from, she didn't want to know. He read from the label.

"Looky here, Grandma. A bottle of Mr. Bubble. And look right here—it's blueberry. And with soothing aloe—oooh. What do you say we get to soothing, Grandma?"

Jimmy carried the roasting pan to the washbasin and ran four inches of warm water in the bottom. He tested the temperature with his finger, approving of its warmth, and took it to her. She held out her hand, motioning for him to bring the pan closer. Sticking her finger into the water, she tested the warmth.

"Why, land sakes, boy," she complained. "I've changed baby diapers hotter than this. If we're really gonna do this, then I want some scalded dogs when I stick my feet in there."

He emptied the water into the washbasin, filling it once more, this time from the hot water tap only. The steam rose, and he was hesitant, afraid he'd burn her. He glanced toward her, thinking about dumping the water in the basin for a third attempt. But before he could act, she waved her hand.

"Well, bring it on, boy. The sun's gonna be setting soon."

He tested the water and pulled his finger back.

"It's too hot, Grandma. It'll burn you."

"You let me be the judge of that," she answered. "Now bring it here, before it gets cold."

He placed the pan on the floor in front of her and opened the bottle, pouring Mr. Bubble into the water, and swishing the blue liquid around with his finger until he could no longer stand the heat. He lifted her foot, hesitating as he held it above the water. She looked him in the eyes, a toughness on her face, and plunged her foot into the bath without a flinch. She felt the burning but shoved the remaining foot in the water. Jimmy stared down at her feet, amazed to see her foot turning red. He slid the pan away from the rocker, inclining her legs to give her more comfort.

The water was hot, enclosing her feet like the waters of the womb. She had plunged into a soothing heaven, and an approving Angel Gabriel knelt before her. The throbbing ceased as the water flowed around her, and she wiggled her toes in the scalding warmth. Her body had caught a chill in the night air and a persistent cold had been with her since. Burn, you devils, she commanded. Burn out the throbbing. Burn out the pain. Burn out the cold of the night. She moved her feet in circles, massaging each ankle with the opposite foot. Steam rose upward, freeing the sweet fragrance of the bubble bath.

"Supposed to smell like blueberries," Jimmy said.

It brought the spring into the room, and she savored the flower-like fragrance rising from the pan. She felt his hands enter the water as it cooled, massaging her feet. Child, may you someday be rewarded for this act of kindness, she said silently, looking down at him.

He raised his head, grinning.

"Hey, look at me, Grandma. I'm washing your feet. Boy, if the guys at school saw me doing this, I'd sure get the ribbing."

"Oliver used to wash my feet like this every now and then," she replied, wiggling her toes, "when my feet hurt from the walking."

She missed her Oliver dearly, the slumbering hollowness buried within her stirred by this loving act of her grandson. Sometimes, when she thought of Oliver, she felt like crying. Tears attempted to well in her eyes, but were forced back at the brink. The world assumed that old people were void of emotion—for they had seen it all—and therefore had no reason to be crying.

"I bet you went through a lot of shoes carrying all that mail around every day, Grandma," Jimmy said, continuing to massage her feet.

"Shoes?" she asked. "You're dead on right about that, boy. I went through a lot of shoes in my day. Never found a pair I really liked, but came close once in awhile. Did so much walking, and shoes didn't seem to last long back then. That's why my feet are so sore and dry now. They just flat got worn out by all that traipsing around. We didn't have fancy jogging shoes back then. They were leather, and some days the bottom of my feet felt like they'd been burned right off from all the pounding they took. You can't imagine how hot two feet can get inside a pair of shoes tramping on burning concrete for eight hours. The skin on my feet used to curl off like corn flakes."

She stopped, reveling in the warmth of the water surrounding her feet. The throbbing in her soles ceased, and her feet relaxed. Her moistened skin was beet red but the impressions dug by the uncomfortable leather were gone, and the chill permeating her body since her trip outdoors had vanished as well.

The warmth of the water relaxed her, tired her, and the fragrance of the bubble bath enveloped her senses. She leaned against the back of the rocker, arms limp on the armrests, and thought of Oliver. The waters disappeared from the pan, and her wrinkled feet grew young once more. Ballroom slippers appeared over youthful feet and she stood up, herself younger now, adorned in a shimmering, blue evening dress. A second pair of shoes appeared, black and shiny, toes pointing toward hers. Oliver stood before her, a handsome young beau. In black tuxedo and top hat, he gracefully slid an arm around her waist. They danced effortlessly around a white floor, blue clouds in the distance, as curious onlookers gazed in admiration. An unseen orchestra played soft, big band music. They twirled through the clouds, unaware of anything else. Their eyes met, becoming one, dancing. Someone stepped on her foot, and she opened her eyes to find Jimmy sitting in the bed, watching her.

"Are you OK, Grandma? You were moving your feet around in the water and hit the edge of the pan. Hope you didn't hurt yourself."

She looked at her feet and to the water slopped on the floor around the pan. Jimmy knelt once more, mopping the spill with a towel.

"It'll be OK, Grandma," he assured her. "Just a little bit on the floor. How do your feet feel now?"

"They feel great, Jimmy. But I wish I could borrow your legs for just a day."

"I wish I could loan them to you, Grandma. You about ready to come out of there?"

She nodded. He pulled one of her feet from the water and placed it on a dry towel.

"I'm kinda feeling like I'm one of the twelve apostles," she said, "with you washing my feet like this. I guess that would make you Jesus."

"I'm a far cry from being Jesus Christ," he grinned, wiping her feet and pointing to his head. "See, my hair's not long enough. But on the other hand, I guess I'd like to be closer to Jesus than the fellow at the other end of the rope."

"Just between you and me, Jimmy, let's keep it that way."

Anna and Jim visited the next day, Saturday.

"Mom, we want you to come over for Thanksgiving."

Her body propped against the pillow, and at the words "come

over" her hands gripped the mattress. Anna saw Viola's muscles tighten.

"Of course, you already know Jimmy's going to be there."

Anna was well aware of her mother's growing fondness for her grandson. It would be OK to leave the raft and go into the water. Viola relaxed her grip.

"I guess it'll be OK," she answered, "if Jimmy's there."

Chapter 13

Viola felt nervous waiting for their arrival. She sat in the rocker, phlegm welling up from the back of her throat. It flowed from deep within as a slick green gel, leaving an acrid taste on her tongue, its presence an embarrassing nuisance. Practically any bodily function she attempted brought embarrassment, but she surrendered, helpless; her simple humanity was pitted against the winds of change with no real hope of victory. She spit the viscous gob from her mouth into a waiting handkerchief. The handkerchief, although fresh, was already saturated.

She looked forward to going to Anna and Jim's home for Thanksgiving, knowing Jimmy would be there, but still grew uncomfortable about leaving. She felt at home in her room, not unlike a jack-in-the-box sealed in his square of space. And she knew to the exact inch where each possession belonged. There were no surprises in her domain. Within these walls she was obliged to no one. Her eyes closed and she visualized the room in her mind, building her universe piece by piece, until the finished mosaic was complete. She opened her eyes and looked around, feeling phlegm rising again. Holding the cloth to her lips, she spit out a wad of gray and realized the handkerchief was too wet to take with her. She eased from the rocker and pulled a fresh one from a stack in one of the drawers. Hesitating, she picked up a second handkerchief. It would be wise to have an extra.

She sat back down, waiting for them to arrive, and looked through the window. Her heart fluttered, the wings of the butterfly, and she pressed a hand against her chest until the fluttering passed. The birdfeeder swayed back and forth, pushed like a swing in the late November breeze and looked lost. For a few mornings following the wren's death, its mate searched the area, chirping with bewilderment on the naked branches of autumn, and then hopping to the birdfeeder to search further when no reply came from the bush. The chirping irritated her, its tone accusing. She felt guilty, for the wren cried out from the branch directly above the dark mound where its mate lay buried. The missing bird had vanished five days before, never to return. The remaining wren, as if sensing evil afoot, fled the bush, returning only sporadically to search for its lost mate. A few sparrows, finding the bush abandoned, now stole food from the birdfeeder, noisily plundering like pirates. She didn't like sparrows—they were loud and dirty, and she banged her cane against the window glass whenever she found them at the birdfeeder.

She glanced at the table where the photos of Oliver and Jimmy sat side-by-side, reminding her how the two were so much alike. Oliver's large photo loomed over the smaller picture of her grandson. But while Oliver's dark wooden frame portrayed a more solemn, stately male, the abstract and wildly colored frame surrounding Jimmy's photo screamed of youth and rebellion. It was fitting that the frame holding each photo defined so well the character within.

The ticking of the wall clock had grown louder—it always did when the battery was running low. She would have to get a new one. A noise in the hallway broke her thoughts, and she turned to find Anna and Jim standing in the doorway.

"Where's Jimmy?" she demanded, gripping the rocker armrests.

"Don't worry, Mom," Anna grinned. "He'll be there, all right. We made the little bugger stay home and clean up his room. We told him that if it wasn't clean when we got home that we'd bring you back here, and he'd miss seeing you on Thanksgiving Day."

"He's sure grown fond of you, Grandma Martin," Jim said.

"Got your bag, Grandma?" Anna asked.

"All set," Viola answered.

Anna insisted that her mother stay with them for the four-day holiday. It would give Viola a chance to get away from the home and spend time with the family. Anna didn't comprehend that after three years of living there, it wasn't "the home" to her mother anymore—it was home. As they prepared to leave, an aide stopped by. She handed Anna four small brown cylindrical bottles.

"Don't forget these," she instructed. "I've put each day's pill in separate bottles, one bottle for each of the four days she'll be gone. That will make it easy. She must take them after the noon meal, with water. It's very important that she take her pills every day."

Anna thanked the aide and dropped the bottles in her purse. She signed her grandmother out for the weekend, and the trio drove to Jim and Anna's home. Viola sat in the back seat, watching in silence as a curious moon appeared, out of place in the blue sky above them. The car sped past the neighborhood where Oliver and she had lived for forty years. The lot where their dream home had once stood was vacant now, the vegetation wearing the rusty browns of late November. The dead grass and dormant shrubbery disappeared, and the house rose from the ground as it had been in its glory, a translucent mirage. Oliver stood on the porch and waved as the car rolled by, and continued waving long after they had passed.

When they opened the front door of Anna's house, Jimmy was waiting for them, an anxious look on his face. The house smelled of roast turkey, and the dining room table was set with Anna's finest china. Jimmy grabbed his grandmother around the neck, giving her a hug as if he hadn't seen her in years.

"Grandma," he greeted. "It's so good to see you."

"Did you clean up your room, you little whipper snapper?" she asked sternly.

"Clean as a whistle," he answered, his face beaming. "Come on in, and I'll show it to you."

He grabbed her hand, pulling her down the hallway as she poked at the floor with her cane.

"Jimmy," Anna yelled, "Don't go so fast. She can't keep up."

Jimmy slowed his pace, and the two disappeared into the boy's room, closing the door behind him while Jim and Anna went to the kitchen to finish preparing the meal.

"You know," Jim said solemnly, "I think your mother's health is failing."

Anna ignored the comment.

"I know you don't want to hear this, Anna," he continued, "but Grandma Martin seems weaker than when we saw her two weeks ago. And I think she's lost a little weight. I think she should see a doctor."

"We've been down this road before, Jim," Anna replied. "She's not going to see a doctor—you know that and I know that. She's stubborn and proud. I'm not going to argue with her again about her health. You know that only stirs her up and her blood pressure shoots up and then she'll be on even more medication, just like last time we tried to help her, doing a lot more harm than good. It hurts me to see her failing, Jim, but we know that's what's going to happen down the road. It's just a fact of life. Just because I don't want to stick her in a hospital doesn't mean that I don't love her. She's my mother. It would break her heart to do that to her now, and we know her heart is already weak. She's going to have to make that decision if she feels she wants to. And don't you even bring it up to her."

"OK," Jim replied, "she's your mother."

"And don't say anything about Grandma's health to Jimmy," she warned. "He doesn't need to know. There's no sense in worrying him, at his age."

Strange noises came from behind Jimmy's closed door.

"Sit down here, Grandma," he said, easing Viola onto a chair in front of his study desk.

He tossed her cane on the bed and handed her a joystick.

"Come on, Grandma, let's have some fun. Let's play a video game."

Jimmy pointed toward the computer screen filled with colorful figures, each moving in a direction that made no sense to her. Jimmy took the joystick from her hands and began shooting at objects moving on the screen.

"You wanna shoot these ones," he instructed, pointing, "but

not these. And don't move too fast toward these blue ones. They blow up and will kill you when they do. Don't shoot these—they're friendlies. And if you get three of these, you get more fuel cells. And then you get to go to the next level. Bigger guns there. Understand, Grandma?"

Unfamiliar to the world of computer games, she took the joystick in hand and began shooting at the screen, randomly and without direction. Time after time her warrior on the screen fell victim to her lack of dexterity and comprehension of the rules of the game. After a few games, however, and with help from Jimmy, she managed to at least hold her own against the computer. As her warrior fought his way around the screen, her body moved with it, twisting when he turned, and ducking when he ducked.

"You're getting into this now, Grandma," Jimmy cheered, watching the game from behind her chair.

Anna and Jim finished preparing the Thanksgiving feast and set all the food on the table. Anna walked down the hall and lifted her hand to knock on Jimmy's closed door, but hesitated, hearing Jimmy and his grandmother laughing inside. When the family had moved back to Minneapolis, Anna had no idea such a strong bond would form between her son and his grandmother. She was pleased the boy opted to visit her every day, when most boys his age were out playing with friends. She listened to the laughter for a few more seconds and rapped on the door.

"Come on out, you two. The turkey is ready."

Viola heard Anna's voice and looked toward the door. When she turned back to the screen, she found her warrior plummeting into a fiery pit.

"Ah, fiddly," she moaned.

Jimmy grinned.

"Don't worry, Grandma. It happens to the best of us."

They feasted at a table covered with turkey and all the trimmings. Anna and Jim sat on one side, and Jimmy and Viola sat across from them.

"How about you saying the blessing, Jimmy?" Anna asked.

"OK," he replied.

He thought for a moment, and stretched his arms out. The four linked hands across the table as Jimmy bowed his head.

"Lord, on this day of Thanksgiving, we want to do just that— say thanks, I mean. We want to thank you for all you have given to us, and all you will give to us. We thank you for our parents and friends. And we thank you for bringing us back home because now we get to see Grandma all the time. Amen."

Jim carved the steaming turkey, and following that, the various bowls filled with the cranberry sauce, sweet potatoes, green beans, and other dishes Anna had spent the morning preparing made their way around the table. Before beginning her meal, Viola reached across the table to Anna.

"Better give me my pills," she said, "before I forget. It's about time."

Anna rose from her chair and retrieved one of the four small bottles from her purse. She handed them to her mother.

"I'll take them after I eat," Viola said, sticking the bottle in her dress pocket.

As they enjoyed their meal, Anna told stories about Jimmy, one of how the boy had once loosened the bolts on the front of his bike when he thought he was tightening them and discovered his mistake when the tire had come off over some railroad tracks, and how he'd arrived at the front door, bleeding and bruised, holding the bike tire and two of his front teeth. Jim discussed some of his projects at work and how he planned to do some traveling after the first of the year. They asked Viola about life at the home, to which she replied that things were going as well as could be expected. When they finished with the main meal, Anna served fresh pumpkin pie with whipped cream.

"Need to take my pills," Viola said. "Then I'm going to take care of some business."

Jimmy, Anna, and Jim watched as Viola put the pills in her mouth, one at a time, swallowing water after each pill, just as the aide had instructed.

"You sure take a lot of pills, Grandma," Jimmy said. It's a good thing you're swallowing them as fast as you're popping them in your mouth."

She nodded, taking another swallow of water. She motioned toward the hallway.

"Down there," Anna said. "The first door to your left."

With the bathroom door closed behind her, Viola bent over the stool, looking into the depths of the water. She glanced defiantly into the mirror, and one by one, spit out the pills she'd trapped beneath her tongue. Each pill fell to the bottom of the bowl. Viola stayed with the family for three more days, spitting her pills into the bowl after each meal.

Chapter 14

It had been a wonderful Thanksgiving with Jimmy, but she was glad to get back to her universe. Familiarity is a good vitamin. Her legs dangled comfortably over the side of the bed as she waited for her grandson to arrive. A fear that he wouldn't come gnawed at her, for the boy and she been together constantly over the last four days.

The loud noise from the clock bothered her since her return. Whether its annoying ticking disturbed her sleep, or she merely imaged it did, she called the custodian to her room to exchange the battery. Two hours later she dragged him back again, complaining that the clock still ticked too loudly, and therefore, she argued, the replacement battery must have been defective. Although the replaced battery was new, the custodian changed it out a second time to appease her. But still, she thought, the second battery was just as weak as the first, for the clock was still ticking too loudly to suit her.

"Hi, Grandma."

Jimmy had arrived, grinning broadly in the doorway.

She felt her heart jump, and hoped it fluttered in joy.

"Did you have a good Thanksgiving?" he asked.

"You ought to know, cocky pup," she shot back. "Weren't you there?"

He grabbed his belly.

"I was, and I'm still full of food. Whatcha doin' anyway?"

"Listening to that darned old clock on the wall."

Jimmy cocked his head, listening.

"I don't hear nothing."

"That's 'cause your ears are all swollen up, listening to all that rock and roll racket you kids call music. It's a wonder you can hear anything at all."

Jimmy moved closer to the clock.

"Sounds fine to me. Just ticking softly, that's all."

He turned his head, listening to sounds coming through the door from outside the room.

"By the way, what's all the commotion out there? There's a bunch of boxes in the hallway."

"Lost my neighbor while I was gone," she explained somberly. "Again."

"Lost?" he asked. "How could she be lost?"

She pointed down the hall.

"Mrs. Warren died in her sleep Friday night."

Jimmy hesitated.

"That's too bad, Grandma. I'm sorry to hear that."

"We weren't close," she replied. "That old bed down there has seen three like her come and go since I moved in here. Now they're all gone. Nobody wants to room next to me anymore."

She spoke her next words almost as if she were proud of them.

"I'm the angel of death, they tell me."

She raised her eyebrows. Jimmy grinned.

"You're an angel, Grandma. That's for sure."

He moved to the window, looking at the birdfeeder.

"Hey, what's that sparrow doing in there?"

He knocked hard on the glass.

"Get outta there! Get off there!"

The bird fled. He turned toward her.

"Where'd they come from? Where are the wrens? If they don't get back here pretty soon those sparrows are going to move in like rats and overrun the place."

The lone wren had failed to appear around the bush or on the birdfeeder since she'd returned to her room the day before.

"I think they've gone south for the winter," she lied. "It may be time to take that feeder down until they come back in the spring. If we don't, that place will be overrun with God only knows what kind of feathered fowl."

"You think?"

"Yes I think. Now go take that contraption down."

"OK, Grandma. If that's what you want, I can do that, no problem."

Jimmy found a stepladder and took down the birdfeeder. He brought it into the room.

"Why don't I store it in our garage for the winter?" he offered. "That way it won't be getting in your way here and I can put it back up in the spring. You've got enough stuff in here right now. And I'm going to bring you some new batteries for your clock tomorrow, too. How does that sound, Grandma?"

Jimmy left a few minutes later, carrying the birdfeeder, the ripping of masking tape echoing from Mrs. Warren's room as a life was boxed and taped for shipment. The following afternoon Jimmy showed up once more, carrying a large brown sack. He put his hand inside the sack.

"I got your batteries," he said, pointing to the clock.

"Must be awful big batteries," she replied. "That's a heck of a sack."

He pulled out the batteries and set the sack aside. Removing the clock from the wall, he exchanged the new batteries for the old.

"There, that should make things a little quieter for you, Grandma."

He picked up the bag.

"Now I have a real surprise for you."

He turned the bag upside down and dumped the contents on the blankets. They were Christmas decorations.

"What are you doing with all that in here?" she barked.

"I'm gonna decorate your room for Christmas," he explained, picking up some of the decorations to show her. "After all, it's gonna be here in less than four weeks. See, I got a big paper nativity scene to hang on your door. And look here, I got this big strand of silver garland—we can put that around that bare old window. I got a little Christmas tree— it's not real, but it's pretty—it's even frosted white. And I got some decorations to put on it."

"And where do you think you're going to put that tree?" she asked.

He looked around the room.

"I'll tell you what," he suggested, "why don't I move that clothes hamper from over in that corner and put the tree on it."

"That's my clothes hamper," she shot back. "Are you daft?"

He held up the paper sack.

"I'll replace it with this then, just until Christmas is over. It's a strong sack. I mean, you don't need nothing fancy to hold dirty clothes, do you?"

He noted her hesitation.

"Oh, come on, Grandma. Be a sport. I've got the tree bought and everything."

His pleading tone and mournful look melted her.

"OK," she teased, "OK, you big baby."

Jimmy jumped up and pulled a roll of Scotch tape from the pile. The colorful nativity scene was large, fully two feet square. He taped it to the front of the hallway door, and stood back to admire the stable where Mary and Joseph hovered over the baby Jesus in the manger as sheep and donkeys stood nearby, watching. He opened the door inward, giving his grandmother a better view.

"See, Grandma. Ain't it pretty?"

The blonde-haired aide who'd cleaned up the broken window glass walked by and stopped to admire the picture. She turned to Viola.

"Oh, Viola, getting ready for the Christmas season already? Looks like you're going to be the first one to get your decorations up this year."

Viola's face beamed.

"Jimmy and me," she answered. "We're decorating for Christmas."

"That's good," the aide replied, winking at Jimmy. "It must be nice to have a grandson who's so thoughtful."

Her wink reaffirmed that he'd been forgiven for the football incident. The aide was pleased by his presence and impressed by the many times the boy visited his grandmother. She continued up the hall as Jimmy moved the wicker hamper to a spot just below the window, sliding the rocker closer to the door.

"Look," he said, satisfied. "Fits real nice right here and the light from the window will shine on it."

He set the tree on the clothes hamper and surrounded the base with a white skirt of felt. Metallic flakes embedded in the cloth reflected light like rays of sun sparkling on newly fallen snow. Jimmy stepped away from the tree, chin in one hand, scrutinizing his work.

"Hmm, this tree looks kinda bare, don't you think, Grandma?"

He opened a smaller sack and tipped the contents onto the mattress.

"You'd be surprised what you can buy at the Post Office these days," he grinned. "Lots more than just stamps."

A dozen Christmas ornaments spilled on the bed, little wrapped packages with United States Postal Service logos on them. The square packages were brilliantly colored, some bearing the Postal Service eagle and others the initials USPS. A white string formed a loop at the top of each ornament.

"Where'd you get the money to buy these things?" she demanded.

"Oh, baby, don't you know I'm loaded?" he shot back, laughing.

Jimmy began hanging the ornaments from the tree, concentrating them on the branches facing the bed and the door. He worked for ten minutes, arranging the decorations, careful that no two ornaments of the same color hung side by side, and then stood back to admire the tree.

"What do you think, Grandma? Pretty neat, huh?"

The late afternoon rays shining through the window fell upon the tree, making the metallic flecks in the cotton skirt sparkle. Her grandson had created an image from her distant past, the sparkling snow over which she'd trod on countless journeys delivering the mail. With the hanging of a few tree ornaments, he'd honored her deeply, whether it had been his intent to or not.

"I like it, Jimmy. I really like it."

She hadn't put up a Christmas tree since moving into the home three years ago.

"Good," he replied. "Now we'll do something about putting some life into this drab old window."

Jimmy spent the next ten minutes winding the long strip of silver garland around the window frame, taping it as he went. When he was finished, the garland took on the look of a picture frame, and the window the portrait inside. Jimmy stored the brown paper sack in the corner where the clothes hamper had been, and left for the day.

She relaxed in bed that evening, tired, and turned her head toward the Christmas tree. Her last conscious memory was that of twinkling flecks of light dancing around the base of the tree.

The second hand turned slowly as she slept, sweeping the face of the clock with the regularity of marching soldiers. Its ticking, silent as her breathing, disturbed her sleep just the same. Her eyes roved sporadically beneath their lids, searching. She woke once, empty eyes alert, but just as quickly surrendering to the darkness. The dream came, the hand moving to press the door buzzer. A white envelope appeared in the hand as the door hinge creaked. She opened the door, a young girl, watching the hand draw closer with the envelope grasped tightly. The slender needle recorded each second.

The dream was different this time. For when she opened the door to reach for the letter, someone stood behind her, blotting out the Christmas tree. Her heart fluttered, and a hand pressed against her chest. Her body jerked and the image fled.

Chapter 15

The dream haunted her the next day, and she remembered it vividly when she woke. With the arrival of the stranger, the dream had changed; and whomever the intruder represented, she was female, slim in statue as Viola's younger self had been at that age. The face was blurred, and the girl was taller than her by half a head. Her mind, shocked by the ominous appearance of this specter, quickly terminated the dream.

She sat in the rocker, facing the hallway. Visitors flocked to her door, drawn by the nativity scene hanging on its face. They peeked through the open doorway in wonder to admire the Christmas tree and garland. Old people she barely knew stopped by, pausing in their wheelchairs or walkers to admire the Christmas decorations, complimenting her, and inquiring from where they had come. Jimmy arrived in the afternoon and added a second strip of tape to a sag in the garland. Disturbed by the frightening change in her dream, she felt she needed to confide in someone.

"I'm waiting for a letter," she said.

Jimmy studied the blank look on her face, confused by her words. She'd already told him this once, and he'd done what he could to get her some mail. He was surprised she'd brought up the subject once more.

"Have you been having that dream again, Grandma?"

She nodded.

"I wouldn't worry too much about it, Grandma. You'll just get yourself all worked up over nothing. It's just a dream. Christmas is coming real soon, Grandma. And you're bound to get lots of letters then. You just wait and see. People dream about weird stuff all the time—especially if they eat something strange. Heck, a couple of nights ago I dreamed that my dad and me switched places and I was my father—weird. Don't want to be my father—I want to be me."

He changed the subject.

"You know, Grandma, you haven't told me any stories for a long time. Why don't you tell me one right now? The heck with that old dream. Tell me a story. It'll make you feel better."

Getting her to tell a story might take her mind off the dream, he thought. His suggestion seemed to work, for she perked up, straightening her shoulders against the back of the rocker. The boy always seemed interested in hearing what she had to say about her past, and she always enjoyed telling him. She had a lot to tell and had kept too much bottled up inside her for too long. It felt re-freshing to let it come out.

"You want to hear a story, boy? You really do?"

"Yea, Grandma, I do."

The boy had grown to savor the stories she told. In that world of memory her face glowed, and a trance-like calm came over her. She looked toward the Christmas tree, reminded of one of her fa-vorite stories.

"Well, since you've gotten so dang hot about Christmas coming, let me tell you a story about what happened one year. It's one of my favorite stories, even if it didn't happen to me."

"Must be a good one, Grandma."

"It's my best one, boy. A long time ago, your great grandfather Clavus worked for the Post Office, way before I did. That's prob-ably how I came to work there, because he did. He told me a story about something that happened to him one Christmas. He used to visit with little kids on his route as he delivered mail. Your great grandfather loved kids—he would have loved to have still been around to see you. Every day along his route kids would walk along beside him and visit. They'd ask him all sorts of things—maybe it was because he was a postman, and they figured he had better ties to the rest of the world than most. He told me once about meeting this little girl who used to sit on the front steps of her house every day, waiting for the mail. She had the cutest grin, he told me. The girl was about eight or nine years old and happy as could be most the time. Even through missing teeth or bruises, she'd always be grinning when he stopped by with the mail. And my dad, your great grandfather Clavus, told me about one day, before Christmas, when he stopped by with the mail, she was sitting on the steps and looking real sad. And this was very unusual for this girl to be like this—he'd never seen her act this way. So he sat down next to her and asked her what was so wrong and how could anybody be so sad. She told my dad that some of the kids at school were teasing her about writing a letter to Santa. She told him that the kids were saying that there was no Santa Claus and that it was just something somebody made up to fool stupid kids."

"There's something awfully familiar about this story, Grandma," Jimmy said, his curiosity aroused. "I think I've heard about that girl."

"Yes, I'm sure you have, Jimmy. Her name was Virginia."

"Well, what did great grandpa tell her?"

"The first thing he asked her is if she'd talked this over with her father. She said she had, and that she'd told her dad that she wanted to write a letter to the newspaper and ask them, because they were really up on things happening in the world and would give her the right answer. She said that her father told her that sounded like a smart idea, and to go ahead and write the letter. And my daddy, sitting on the step beside her that day, said that it sounded like a pretty good idea, too. He even offered to personally take the letter to the office of the *New York Sun* and deliver it himself, if she'd just write it."

"And she did," Jimmy said.

"Yes, she wrote the letter all right, just like she said she would. And your Great Grandfather Clavus walked it right into the newspaper office and told them to make sure it was read—that the letter meant a great deal to a very special little girl on his mail route. And the editor did read it, and was so impressed with what the girl said that he wrote a long reply called 'Yes, Virginia, there is a Santa Claus.' And it was printed up in the paper. The editor told her not to worry about what her friends were saying—that they were wrong, and that the world truly needed somebody like Santa Claus. Everybody loved the editor's response to Virginia's letter. In fact, the response was so popular it was run in newspapers all over the country for years after that. And still does."

"And Great Grandfather Clavus was the one who delivered Virginia's letter to the newspaper?" Jimmy asked. "That's a great story, Grandma. Did Great Grandfather Clavus ever tell anyone about what he did?"

"Only to a few, Jimmy. Just me and maybe one or two others."

"Why?"

"I guess he didn't want people finding out he'd helped the girl, because the story was so good without him in it."

Jimmy pondered the story for a moment.

"Well, I wonder what ever became of Virginia?"

He stood before Mr. Tyler's history class two days later, his voice full of excitement. Anxious to pass on this bit of history his grandmother had told him, he'd researched the story further.

"And Virginia went on to college and became a schoolteacher. And then she became a school principal."

"That is a very interesting story, Jimmy," Mr. Tyler said, sitting on the edge of his desk. "Most unusual to hear a side story on such an important piece of history that's not in most history books. And since we're entering the Christmas season, the story is most appropriate now."

"I suppose you're going to write a letter to the newspaper now, too," a dark-haired girl sitting in the front row teased. "To Santa."

Her name was Amelia Hernandez, and Jimmy had met her when he'd started school in September. Like Jimmy, she was new to the school. Amelia had the thickest black hair Jimmy had ever seen, and shiny eyes as dark as coal. She was OK, for a girl, he'd concluded.

"Yea," Howard piped in, "maybe Jimmy can ask about Santy

Claus, too. And then we can all find out if you've been a good boy all year long."

"Oo-oo-ooh, Jimmy," several voices teased from around the room.

"Jimmy's been a bad boy this year," Trevor added, encouraged by his classmates barbs. "He ain't getting nothing for Christmas."

Trevor couldn't understand why Jimmy preferred to spend so much time with his grandmother when he could be playing football, bike riding, or even throwing stones into the nearby creek. Trevor perceived himself to be unimportant in Jimmy's eyes after the final bell rang. He resented his classmate who seemed to value their friendship only during the school day. He thought that was the shallowest kind of friendship.

Jimmy rested on his bed that evening, hands tucked behind his head, thinking. He remembered Amelia's words and a plan began to form in his mind. More than anything, he wanted his grandmother to get her letter. If she did, perhaps her dream would go away. He grinned as he thought of his plan. Rising in the darkness, he clicked on the desk lamp next to his bed. Rummaging through the top drawer, he found a pad of paper and a pen, he hunched over the desk, thinking. He hesitated, picking his words, and set pen to paper, scribbling as the hands of the clock raced toward midnight. He would have to hurry, for Christmas would soon be upon them.

In her room that same evening, Grandma Martin had already finished her work. She grinned as the second hand ticked away. Scissors in hand, she cut a piece of aluminum foil, snipping at sharp angles. She had a bit of a surprise for her cocky pup of a grandson as well.

Chapter 16

That afternoon Viola had been surprised to find a different aide stopping at her doorway with the rolling cart. The girl was younger than the regular aide, barely out of high school. Peppy and optimistic, her motion was quick but jerky, like those of the wrens. The regular aide, she told Viola, had taken a week off to visit a sick relative in Wisconsin. She made small talk as she wrapped the blood pressure band around Viola's arm and pumped the bulb to tighten the band around her bicep.

The aide continued to chatter away, unaware that her patient was sizing her up. She finished taking Viola's vital signs and returned to the cart. Searching the row of bottles, she brought back the day's pills. Viola accepted her handful, popping the first hungrily into her mouth. She asked the aide for a cup of water, and when the girl's back was turned, Viola slid her remaining pills into her pocket. The aide returned with the water and Viola pointed to her mouth, holding out an empty palm.

"Oh, you shouldn't take them all at once like that, Mrs. Martin," she warned. "You might choke."

Viola motioned for the water, opening her mouth to show a pill. Satisfied, the aide gave her the water.

"Let's be more careful tomorrow and not stick all those pills in your mouth at once, please," she cautioned, "or I might get into trouble. And we wouldn't want that, would we, Mrs. Martin?"

"Tomorrow I'll be more careful," Viola promised, swallowing hard. "I wouldn't want a nice girl like you getting in trouble over some old war horse like me."

She'd be more careful the next day. There was no reason not to, for she'd gotten what she'd sought and needed no more.

She held the aluminum foil she'd taken from the cafeteria,

cutting carefully with the scissors. With the floor lamp throwing its tight beam of light, she felt a bit like a criminal. But the feeling excited her. She worked slowly yet methodically, kneeling next to the bed, her elbows braced against the mattress. Five tiny pills huddled on the bedspread. She finished cutting the foil into a six-pointed star and placed it on the bed. She grabbed a cardboard star she'd cut earlier and laid it on foil, bending the foil inward. Picking up a pill, she set it near one point of the cardboard star and folded the foil over the cardboard. A silver bump was visible where the foil concealed the pill. She repeated the task five more times, until all the points of the star were covered with aluminum foil, a tiny pill hidden beneath.

When the shiny star was viewed from the front, its surface was smooth. Only she knew of the secret behind each silver point. The Star of Bethlehem had shone through the night, giving life to a cold world. When she made the star, she decided to extend it life, to share with the Light of the World some small part of what was her—the tiny pills that kept her heart in life.

Jimmy walked in that afternoon and spotted the star gleaming from the top the Christmas tree.

"Hey, Grandma," he said excitedly, "Look at that star. Did you make that?"

"I did," she replied. "And what is it to you if I did?"

"Nothing. Hey, I think it's pretty neat. When did you do this?"

"What'd think? That I just sit around all day waiting for you to show up? You don't think I can do anything for myself?"

"Oh, no, Grandma. That's not it at all. I just think it's great that you did that all by yourself. You see, you can get in the Christmas spirit. I bet you're the only person in this whole building who's made their own Christmas star. I bet everybody's gonna be jealous now and start decorating up their own rooms for the holidays. You're gonna be the ambassador of Christmas this year, Grandma. That's what we'll call you. Grandma Martin, the Ambassador of Christmas."

"You'll do no such thing, cocky pup."

He grinned.

"Hey, since you're in the Christmas spirit, how about if me and some of my friends come over and sing you some Christmas songs? You know, to kinda get you in the mood of the season. I know they'd love to sing for you. We could do a little vaudeville, baby, too."

He shuffled across the room, dancing. Hands open and facing the floor, he moved his arms with a jerky in and out motion away from his body.

It had been a long time since someone had made her such an offer. The idea sounded delightful, for the thought of young voices raised in song pleased her as much as the symphonies of songbirds she'd created on her own. But the songbirds had ceased with the departure of the widowed wren. She remembered how she had walked the halls with Jimmy during his Valenteen holiday, passing out candies to those who had nothing. She remembered how some had pawed the air like dogs doing tricks, silently begging for the two of them to remain in their rooms to ease the pain of being left behind. For these silent ones, young voices filled with song would be a godsend.

"I'll tell you what, Grandson, I'll do you one better. Why don't you come on over and just sing out for everybody?"

Her remarked stunned him, and he stopped shuffling.

"Everybody? What do you mean by that?"

She swept her arm in a wide arc, scooping her hand as it moved back and forth across her body.

"I mean the whole darn place. Everybody."

"Now wait a minute, Grandma. I don't like being in front of crowds all that much. And I'm really not a very good singer. And I don't know if my friends—"

She stared at him coldly.

"You telling me you're all talk, boy? You all wind, are you?"

Jimmy was dumbstruck. She pointed a thumb at her body, jerking her fist back and forth.

"I'm the Ambassador of Christmas—those are your words, boy,

not mine. And the Ambassador of Christmas wants to hear some singing in her home. And she'd like to hear that singing pretty gall darn soon. So what are you going to do about it, Mr. Brag Himself Up? Or are you just all talk?"

The boy glanced toward the homemade star twinkling on the apex of the Christmas tree and then gazed back to the rocker. For an instant it appeared as a throne, and she the queen she claimed to be. His offer to sing had been, in actuality, a jest. He never dreamed his grandmother, so tightly wound in the world of her room, would want her universe to be invaded by a group of noisy twelve-year-olds. He hadn't asked any of his friends about singing, and didn't know if they'd come even if he did. But his crafty grandmother had turned the tables on him.

"I'll see what I can do," he replied sheepishly.

"I'll be waiting," the ambassador replied.

At school the following morning he stopped Amelia in the hallway.

"Amelia," he began, "I know you're in the school chorus…"

To his relief, Amelia volunteered to sing with him when he told her about his grandmother's request. She was talented, played the piano well, and had a lovely singing voice. Trevor and Howard, however, were tougher nuts to crack.

"This is gonna cost you," Trevor said, sniffing opportunity.

"I'll take you to a movie," Jimmy offered. "We'll go, and it'll be my treat. Tickets and everything you eat."

"What's in it for me?" Howard demanded. "If you want me to go to the old folk's home and sing a bunch of songs in front of a bunch of old fogies, it had better be something real good. Something worth my while."

"What do you want?"

Howard stared into Jimmy's eyes.

"Your bike. I'll take your bike."

"My bike? You want my bike?"

Howard's request surprised Jimmy. He looked down at the bike he straddled as the trio stood on top of the hill overlooking the retirement home. The bike was new only four months before and his most prized possession. He rode it to see his grandmother almost every day.

"If you want me to sing in front of a bunch of old fogies, then fork over the wheels," Howard said firmly. "That's my deal."

"OK, OK," Jimmy agreed reluctantly. "But for a bike you'd better be singing like the Vienna Boys Choir."

They gathered at the retirement facility two weeks before Christmas, after practicing several afternoons in the school music room. The staff crowded dozens of senior citizens in the lounge area, where rows of chairs had been arranged before a piano. Jimmy stood rigidly in front of the piano, the tip of a red and white Santa hat dangling over the side of his head. Trevor and Howard, also wearing Santa hats, and visibly nervous, stood behind the piano, as if trying to hide.

"This is so stupid," Trevor said, watching the crowd grow as he eyed the "Exit" sign over a door. "Why did I let you talk me into this?"

"A deal's a deal," Jimmy reminded him. "Too late to back out now."

Each time one of the boys turned their head, the little white ball on the tip of their hat followed, as if trying to catch up. Amelia, brimming with confidence, and ecstatic with being in front of an audience, sat on a bench at the piano keyboard. A green and red elf's hat with a silver bell attached to its tip adorned her head, and a wrist bracelet of small gold bells jingled each time she moved her hands.

When the crowd finished gathering, one of the aides addressed them, pointing toward Viola.

"We have a real special treat for you today, folks, as we near the holidays. Viola Martin's grandson, Jimmy Paige, has brought a few of his friends over to sing some Christmas carols for us."

Jimmy scanned the faces before him. This is like winter, he thought. Almost every person had hair of pure white, as if on each head, a gentle snow had fallen. The younger staff members were easy to pick out, and one rotund aide with a huge mop of red hair stood out particularly prominent in the sea of white. Some elders wore new clothing, recently retrieved from the dry cleaners just for the occasion, and many of the women had their hair neatly permed. Others wore only a housecoat and slippers. Some were shaking, unable to control their motions. Barely able to comprehend what was about to happen, they were the lost sailors on the sea. Viola was seated on the couch in the front row, in the midst of three other elderly women. Her little body, floating on the large cushions, made her appear more like a child's doll than a person. Jimmy stepped forward.

"Merry Christmas, everybody. My name is Jimmy Paige and I'm here today with my friends Howard, Trevor, and Amelia to share some Christmas songs with you. We hope you like them."

Jimmy nodded toward Amelia, and she began playing the piano. Their first song was "We Wish You A Merry Christmas." As they began singing, they grimaced when certain notes emerged from the badly out-of-tune piano. They sang off-key at times, their voices clashing with the sour piano notes. But they merely sang louder when this occurred, drowning out the piano. The crowd listened, mesmerized by flawed notes and off-key voices. Old bones ceased their shaking and vacant eyes found solace in memories culled from long ago.

They sang "Grandma Got Run Over By a Reindeer" next, their voices excited and faces happy as the crowd howled at the fate of the unfortunate grandmother. Amelia banged away on the piano, the bell on her elf hat jiggling as her head rocked back and forth, her black eyes dancing. Her elf cap flopped back and forth, clinging for dear life to her gleaming black hair. Trevor caught Jimmy's eye, admitting with facial gestures that maybe this singing wasn't such a bad idea after all. The crowd clapped eagerly when the song ended. Jimmy asked if everyone had been good boys and girls all year, and the rotund red-haired aide, her hands gripping the back of a wheelchair, replied that most of them had been exceptionally good and that they were all anxious for St. Nick to arrive.

Jimmy announced that the next song was to be "O Holy Night" and asked the audience to sing along. As the soft notes rose, old people who hadn't shown a hint of sanity for months began to sing. An old woman in the corner sang feebly. Her voice rose with the purity she'd sung years ago in the church choir; but those around her had until now only heard broken mutterings, ramblings from a mind that no longer functioned. Throughout the room worn voices joined, singing about this special holy night. An old man near the front shook uncontrollably, dribble from his mouth soaking the front his shirt. The red-haired aide continued to grip the handles of the wheelchair as the occupant tried to roll toward the singers. The man searched the floor, trying to locate the brick in front of his tank tread. His nickname was "Racecar" because he liked to run his wheelchair up and down the hall as fast as he could and occasionally required restraining.

As the song ended, Amelia looked at Jimmy, her eyes flashing with delight. Jimmy glanced to Trevor and Howard and noted that the two were enjoying themselves. They continued, singing "Jingle Bells" and "Dashing Through The Snow" without pausing, and moving on to "It's Beginning To Look a Lot Like Christmas" and "Silent Night." Amelia's piano went silent and Jimmy spoke.

"We've written a special song we'd like to sing for you today, just because we heard you've all been so good this year. We wrote it just for you. We call the song 'It's Christmas' and we hope you like it."

He smiled and winked at his grandmother. As Amelia played the music she'd composed, they sang the simple lyrics Jimmy had penned.

It's Christmas
Just like it was before
Bring back those days from memory
Bring them back to me once more

It's Christmas

115

The tree so high and bright
A star to guide you onward
A beam of hope and light

It's Christmas
You're young and foolish free
Your heart is filled with laughter
And the world sings happily

It's Christmas
Remember those before
Remember all those happy times
And call them back once more

As the final notes died, the crowd applauded. One of the aides stepped in front of the piano as the clapping ceased. A table filled with refreshments was wheeled into the lounge.

"Thank you very much, Jimmy, and Jimmy's nice friends. It's so nice to hear the sound of young voices. But now, we appear to have a bit of a problem, though. It looks as though someone has left a mountain of goodies on that table over there, and we desperately need some volunteers to eat them."

"Hey, that wasn't so bad," Trevor grinned as they gathered around the table a few minutes later. He munched on a mouthful of cookies while cramming more into his coat pockets to take with him. "And we sounded pretty good."

"Yea," Howard bragged. "They loved us."

"Yea, they loved us," Amelia grinned sarcastically, "because most of them can't even hear. They couldn't tell how bad you guys really sounded."

Amelia shot Howard a long, hard stare. His face flushed and he stopped chewing on his cookie.

"OK, OK," he said, turning to face Jimmy. "Jimmy, I guess you can just go ahead and keep your dumb old bike."

Chapter 17

The letter addressed "Editor" arrived at the office of the *Minneapolis Star* two days after Jimmy mailed it. One of dozens delivered that afternoon, the plain white envelope lay abandoned on the corner of a cluttered desk for half a day. The resident of the desk, the Chief Editor, finally opened the envelope. He drew a yawn and began reading the crude writing set to paper under the dim light of a desk lamp.

Dear Mr. Editor:

My name is Jimmy Paige and I hope you're having a wonderful Christmas season. I am. I think it's a time for joy, and a time for all of us to be grateful for all the things we have. And I think it's a wonderful time to think about what we could do for others right now.

I have a way, I think, of helping out my grandmother. She is so wonderful. She's in an old folks home right now. And that's OK, because she likes it there so much. She has her own room, and I get to go over and see her every day because she lives right next to my school. She tells me stories all the time about herself and all the things she did during her life. She worked for the Post Office for fifty years, you know, so she has lots of stories to tell. She carried mail to so many people, for so many years, and made lots of people happy when she came to their door to give them their letters.

The trouble is, now she doesn't hardly get any mail anymore, for herself I mean. I think that makes her very sad because she tells me once in awhile that she'd like to get some. The other night she told me the story about Virginia, the girl who wrote a letter to the *New York Sun* a long time ago, asking about Santa Claus, and how

117

her father was the one who delivered the letter to the editor way back in 1897. This gave me an idea that I hope you will help me with. My grandmother says she's waiting for a letter, but none ever comes in the mail for her so I think she gets very lonely sometimes. I do the best I can, but I can't be there all the time. I was wondering if you could put something in your newspaper, telling people to send my grandmother a Christmas card so she'd have something to read and to know people still care. I would greatly appreciate if you would do this. You see, my grandmother spent so much of her life trying to make people happy by bringing them letters from their loved ones that I'd like to see her get some mail that would make her happy. She doesn't get out much and it would mean so much to her. If you would put her address in your newspaper, and ask people to write to her, it would make her very happy. Her address is: Viola Martin, Friendship Retirement Home, New Elmwood, Minnesota.

Merry Christmas,

Jimmy Paige

The editor read the letter again, pressing a finger to his lips as he propped one foot against his desk. Spotting a co-worker, he waved her over.

"Hey, Julie. How about doing me a favor?"

He circled the name and address at the bottom of the letter.

"Check to see if this information is correct, will you?"

He handed her the letter, and she turned away, reading it.

"New Elmwood," she said, turning back, "that's only ten miles down the road."

The editor returned to the stack of paper on the desk. He'd been so busy that he hadn't torn the calendar page for two days. Christmas was less than two weeks away, and he hadn't done a bit of shopping.

Viola sat in the rocker that evening, watching television. The soles of her feet throbbed, and she wished Jimmy were there to soak her feet with the warm bubbly water that smelled like flowers.

She leaned against the back of the rocker, eyes closed, imagining her feet immersed in the soothing waters, so intent that she lifted one foot to test the temperature. Her eyes opened as a voice spoke. An old black and white movie played on the television. A piercing wind blew around the flowing robes of a transparent specter as an old man cringed before it, terrified. The old man shivered in the winter cold as he told the specter of the great fear he had of its presence. She watched with blank eyes as the specter led Scrooge through a field of tombstones, begging to be told if the images he was seeing were things that would be or things that only might be. She recalled the specter from her own dream as snow fell around Scrooge and the Ghost of Christmas Yet to Come. She pressed the remote to change the channel to the evening news.

She winced as she felt her heart jump with a pinprick of pain. The ticking of the clock boomed over the voice of the female reporter as she spoke to the anchorman back in the newsroom. Her frosty breath swirled around the microphone she clutched in one hand. A house smoldered behind her, pouring smoke into the night sky as a gentle snow fell.

"Ken, we are here in Eden Grove tonight, one of many suburbs clustered in southwest Minneapolis. As you can see, an intense fire has completely engulfed this house at 72 Guesner Street in a little less than thirty minutes. The fire broke out shortly after eight tonight and quickly gutted the entire structure."

"Katie," the anchorman asked, "Have you been able to determine the amount of damage done to the house? It looks pretty bad from where I'm sitting."

"The house appears to be a total loss," she replied. "The fire apparently began with a gas leak in the kitchen and exploded, setting off this devastating inferno. Fortunately the mother, Mrs. Lois Hernandez, and two of her children, Amelia, twelve, and Rachael, four, were in the family room at the time of the explosion. That was fortunate for them, for that may have been what saved their lives. The family room was located in the basement, and the floor separating the two rooms shielded the mother and the two girls from the blast. Mrs. Hernandez and her children were able to escape, literally, just seconds before the flames blocked the doorway leading from the basement, which was the only way out of the house."

"Was anyone else in the house at the time, Katie?"

"Yes, seven-year old Paul Hernandez broke his leg when he was forced to jump from the second story window as the fire began to engulf the upstairs bedrooms. The boy has been taken by ambulance to Minneapolis General Hospital, and we understand that Mrs. Hernandez has accompanied him there. The other two children remain here and are in the care of neighbors. And as you can see behind me, Ken, the house is a total loss."

The screen filled with the smoldering image of a piano visible through blackened two-by-four wall studs.

"Was anyone else living in the house, Katie?" the anchorman asked.

"Yes, Ken. Mr. John Hernandez, the father of the family, was at the airport picking up his parents who'd just arrived from Mexico City to spend the Christmas holiday with their three grandchildren. This visit was the first time the grandparents had ever seen their grandchildren. When Mr. Hernandez arrived home with them a short time ago, he found his house totally engulfed in flames."

"What was his initial reaction when he saw the fire, Katie?"

"As you can imagine, Ken, his first concern was for his family, and he attempted to run into the inferno to save them. He had to be restrained by police and firefighters who, over all the noise and confusion, tried to get him to understand that his family was already out of the house."

"Where's the family now, Katie?"

"We understand that some of the neighbors have volunteered to help out the family, and the Red Cross has also offered temporary shelter to the family. We have asked Mr. Hernandez to speak with us for a few moments."

She motioned toward a group of people watching the house

smolder. A short, dark-haired man, black soot on his face, came forward to speak with the reporter as firefighters sprayed water on isolated islands of rising smoke.

"Ken, this is John Hernandez, owner of the house."

She turned, addressing the man, and held the microphone between them.

"Mr. Hernandez, may I first tell you how extremely sorry we are for what has happened to you and your family, especially in light of the fact that this tragedy occurred so close to the Christmas holidays. I understand your seven-year-old son Paul sustained a broken leg during his jump out the upstairs window, but that he'll be OK, and the rest of your family is safe, and we thank God for that. What did you think when you saw the fire as you drove up?"

Viola watched, wiping her mouth with a moist handkerchief. As she listened, she felt the fluttering again, butterflies against her heart.

The man, stunned, replied.

"I was horrified. My whole life went before me. I wouldn't know what to do if I lost my family. And my parents were with me, watching as I was. This is their first visit to see us from Mexico. I told them while we rode from the airport how we'd saved our money and bought the house, and how proud we were to own it. They were as horrified as I was when we drove up and saw the fire burning everything."

The reporter spoke, glancing down at her notes.

"An interesting side story about Mr. Hernandez, Ken, is that he is originally from Mexico, having arrived in the United States fifteen years ago, not knowing how to speak English. He later joined the United States Army, saw action in Desert Storm, and obtained United States citizenship. He and Mrs. Hernandez waited five years, saving enough for the down payment on this house. They moved into this house only about six months ago, and then began saving money to bring his parents from Mexico to

Minneapolis for Christmas, only to have them find his house burning to the ground."

Behind the reporter, the man's parents huddled in the lights of the camera, a blanket hanging from their shoulders.

"What are your plans now, Mr. Hernandez?" the reporter asked. "What are you going to do?"

"I don't know," the man replied. "Everything is gone—our house, our clothes, everything. We even bought all our Christmas presents early because we wanted to spend all our vacation time with my parents."

The man nodded toward the smoldering cloud snaking its head along the ground in the night air.

"All the presents were in the attic. Everything we'd bought—gone."

Viola's face stared blankly at the TV screen as the camera fell upon the man's children watching the fire. She recognized the older girl's face in the glow, the dark hair and shiny black eyes, remembering how the girl had banged away on the piano a few days before as she sang Christmas carols. The little girl's piano now stood among a forest of charred wall studs, burned beyond use.

The old woman changed the channel to find Scrooge kneeling in the cold, wiping snow away from a gravestone with his sleeve. She had no fear of the Ghost of Christmas Yet to Come, as Scrooge had. She knew him quite well, as a matter of fact, and would be his maker.

Chapter 18

Buried in the rubble of the evening editorial of the *Minneapolis Star*, the last paragraph read:

And to anyone out there burning with the holiday spirit, we have a special request from a twelve-year old boy for his grandmother, a retired mail carrier. The boy writes to tell us that his grandmother lives by herself in a retirement home and is very anxious to get some Christmas mail. What do you say, readers? Got a Christmas card to spare? Want to spread some cheer? If you'd like to make one of our senior citizens feel a little more appreciated during this holiday season, send a Christmas wish to: Viola Martin, Friendship Retirement Home, New Elmwood, Minnesota.

Viola sat contentedly in the rocker, waiting for the arrival of the aide. She grew impatient watching the clock, but conceded that it was her own apprehension and not the tardiness of the aide that disturbed her. She rocked slowly back and forth, her cane resting across her thighs. She heard the cart rolling down the hallway. The aide, returning from her trip to Wisconsin, appeared in the doorway.

"Viola," she said, "It's so good to see you again. And look at you—why you look like the cat who ate the canary."

She noticed the envelope in the old woman's hand.

"What are you up to, Viola?"

"Can't a body post a gall darned letter without somebody making a big fuss over it?" she snapped.

"Well, I guess you can," the aide replied. "But I've never

known you to ever send a letter out to anyone. What are you trying to do, Viola, win the lottery?"

"No," Viola snorted. "But can't I can send a Christmas card just like anybody else? And without any permission from you or anybody else, I hope."

The aide smiled. As Viola's excitement grew, she rocked back and forth with increasing vigor.

"You can do whatever you like, Viola," the aide assured her. "Of course you can. Would you like me to mail that for you so you won't have to walk down the hall to the mail drop?"

Viola had turned the television off late the previous evening, the plight of the family who'd lost everything gnawing at her. She sat in the darkness for a long time, thinking. The girl who'd visited with Jimmy gifted them unselfishly with music and song, bringing back memories of Christmases long since faded. And now the girl and her family would have no Christmas.

A bird flew past the window as she rocked, stirred from its slumber by the prowling of a cat. Its shadow, outlined by moonlight, floated across the bedspread to fall upon her body. Pinned for an instant against her heart, the shadow disappeared into the night, the bird seeking refuge far from the cat. The bird's shadow reminded her of the darkness below the bush; the secret buried in the cold earth. Perhaps the shadow had been the soul of the wren, borrowed from the grave to guide her. Unlike the soul beneath the bush, she would rise from the darkness, to bring light.

She stood up, closing the hallway door until only a sliver of the light shone from a crack beneath the threshold. She retrieved her stamp binder and opened it, paging through the memories held inside. She studied the book until time collapsed, so engrossed with reminiscing that she forgot the reason she'd opened the book in the first place. The pages opened before her, each holding treasures from her past, a summation of her time spent on earth. In the faint light bouncing from her eyeglasses, history reaffirmed itself in the minute squares. Presidents passed before her, staring stoically from the face of the stamps. Heroes, explorers, and inventors marched past, her eyes acknowledging the greatness of their achievements. She feasted on birds and animals, each held tightly in their little paper cage. Flowers painted with such realism that her nostrils quivered at the fragrance brought her immense pleasure. She smiled at the irony as she scanned the pages of flawed stamps, their value rising above the perfect merely because they were imperfect. She turned another page, finally finding what she'd opened the binder seeking.

She rummaged around for some time, scrounging for a Christmas card and an envelope, two actually. She managed to find a card with a brightly decorated tree on its face. Viola wrote a short greeting inside, her hand unsteady as she scrawled the words. Satisfied with what she'd penned, she raised her head, staring at the far wall, thinking. She lowered her head, chuckling, and added a signature below the greeting. She slipped the card into the small envelope, and slid the smaller envelope into a larger one, scribbling the address she'd heard just once, on TV. She had seen thousands of addresses during her time, and memorizing one more was simple. She placed a stamp on the upper right corner and sealed the envelope.

The aide repeated her question, pointing.

"Viola, would you like me to mail that for you?"

"OK," she replied cautiously. "But make darn sure you do."

She surrendered the envelope, irritated when the card was left unattended among the forest of pill bottles on top of the cart. But she said nothing, trusting in her Maker that things would get done the way He wished them to be done. The aide recorded her vital signs, raising her eyebrows.

"Blood pressure is up again, Viola."

"If you got poked and prodded as much as I did, girlie," she answered tartly, "your dander would be up, too."

When she got excited, her blood pressure always rose, as it did now, with the outbound mail.

"You don't forget to mail that," she said, pointing her cane toward the cart.

The aide picked up the envelope.

"You forgot the return address, Viola."

"Don't need one. Just mail it off."

Two hours later the aide returned, handing her an envelope.

"You told me you were going to mail it for me," Viola scolded, refusing the envelope. "And you didn't do it."

"Settle down, Viola," she answered. "I mailed it off like you asked, just a few minutes ago. The mailman just came and took it. But this letter came for you."

"What?"

"It looks like a Christmas card," the aide said. "Postmarked Bemidji."

"Hells bells, I don't know anybody in Bemidji. Not a soul. Why would anybody be sending me anything from there?"

"Well, Viola, I guess you'll just have to open it up and see."

The aide placed the envelope on Viola's lap and left the room. Viola picked the card up, looking first at the stamp. She admired the brightly colored Christmas tree, pretty even through the black ripples of the cancellation stamp. She looked for flaws, but found none. On the upper left hand corner, the name and address of the sender had been affixed with a preprinted label. The name "Erickson" was unfamiliar to her, and she wondered about the mysterious sender as she tore open the envelope and pulled out the card. A picture of the nativity scene greeted her, an oversized star gleaming so brightly in the blue sky above the stable that she could feel the warmth from each ray. Shepherds and animals faced the stable, watching, giving the impression that she was peering over their shoulders into the very bosom of the manger. The images were raised, like Braille, so life-like anyone seeing the card might feel as if they, too, were there with that small gathering on that cold winter's night. Viola opened the card to the standard printed greeting. Below the print, a handwritten message had been added:

Dear Viola,

Wishing you the best at Christmastime, from our home to yours. May your holiday season be filled with joy and peace, and may God bless and protect you in all you do.

Best wishes,

Jim and Loretta Erickson

Fellow Mail Carrier (Retired)

She read the message over several times and turned the card to admire the nativity scene again. She searched her memory, trying to find some significance in the name, some fragment of information from the past. Who were these people? Where had their paths crossed? Had he been a fellow postal worker with her long ago? The family name was common enough throughout Minnesota. She tapped the card against her hand, puzzled. Try as she did, no answer came to her.

She felt a cough coming, and instinctively reached for her handkerchief, waiting for the upwelling of phlegm. Her heart skipped and then felt heavy.

Chapter 19

Jimmy sat on the bed, hanging his head.

"It's almost Christmas," she said. "What's the matter, boy?"

"I'm so sad, Grandma," he answered. "Some things are just so unfair."

"You're just finding that out, are you? Maybe there is hope for you after all, boy."

"Don't tease me today. Just please don't."

"Well, tell your old grandma why a healthy boy like you is so glum then."

He raised his head to look at her.

"I wasn't going to tell you this," he began, "but I might as well. It's about my friend Amelia. She's new at school this year. She's the girl who came over to sing with us last week. Her house caught on fire four nights ago and burned to the ground. Everything they have is gone. She hasn't even been in school the last few days. They don't have any money and I'm scared for her. Her grandparents came here from Mexico to spend Christmas with them, and their house burned down. Now they're staying at the Red Cross shelter. What a lousy deal."

"That's too bad," she said, almost casually. "But I'm sure things will work out for them."

He looked at her, angry.

"How can you say that, Grandma? How can you be so nonchalant about something like this? You don't understand. Nothing's gonna work out. They're poor, Grandma. They lost everything—everything they had. They have nothing. Don't you understand that? It's not fair that this had to happen to them, especially right at Christmas time."

"You're going to find out that a lot of things in this life ain't fair, boy. When that happens you just got to trust in the Lord, Jimmy. He'll work it out for them, I expect."

He stared at her, unbelievingly.

"How can you even think that, Grandma? What's to become of those poor people, huh? I go to church every Sunday and nobody has ever come down the aisle in there and handed me anything. And now you're talking like God is going to stroll right through that door over there."

"Don't ever underestimate His power," she answered. "The Lord comes through many doors, even those in which He is not always welcome."

"Well," Jimmy huffed, "you believe what you want, Grandma. But all I know is that Amelia and her family are going to have a lousy Christmas. And through no fault of their own. For all I know, they may have to move away and I'll never get to see her again. And she's so nice. I was just getting to know how nice she really is."

Jimmy left a half hour later. His anger boiled at his grandmother's complacency regarding Amelia's plight, and he marched indignantly from the building. Ten minutes later the aide visited Viola, handing her five envelopes.

"You're pretty popular today, Viola," she winked.

She was surprised at the volume of mail. Each envelope was postmarked from a different town and bore the return address of someone she couldn't recall knowing. She pulled a brightly colored Christmas card from each envelope, reading the written message aloud. Her voice whispered with joy.

Viola,
Wishing you the best at Christmas time.
Bill and Julie Donaldson, Cokato

Viola,
May your Christmas be filled with every joy and happiness.
The Paulicks, Eden Prairie

Viola,

Across the miles, here's wishing you the best at Christmas.

Rose, Rose Wilson Hair Salon

P.S. If you ever get to Willmar, come in for a free perm.

Viola,

Many blessings to you during this holiday season. May you be filled with the joy of the season and welcome the Light of the World into your heart.

Sister Elizabeth Hogan, Albert Lea

Viola,

Peace to you during this holiday season.

Donna Landers, Minneapolis

When she finished reading, she stacked the cards on her lap and leaned her back against the rocker, smiling contently. She didn't understand why strangers were sending her cards, but she hoped they kept coming.

Jimmy visited the following day.

"Sorry I was such a grouch yesterday, Grandma."

"Have you thought about what I said?"

"Yes, Grandma. And I suppose you're right. Things will work out for the best. But I don't know if God's going to help out any, but I guess it's not gonna hurt to tell Him about it at least. Amelia was back at school today, anyhow, and I got to see her. The Red Cross is giving them a place to stay for awhile."

"Feel a little better now, do you?"

"Yes, Grandma, I do. As a matter of fact..."

He handed her a present wrapped neatly with Christmas paper.

"Yea, I know it's early, but I want to give it to you now so you can enjoy it during the Christmas season. I know it's your favorite time of year."

"You know why it's my favorite time of year, Jimmy? Because all through my life I got to make so many people happy when I delivered them mail at Christmas. I mean, the rest of the year was fine, but everyone was so excited at Christmas when I used to come to their door. Sometimes that's the only time friends heard from each other, but it seems that that one time made all the difference between knowing and not knowing. It always made me proud to see their faces light up when they read the return address, knowing that somebody they hadn't heard from in almost a year had sent them a card. "

She removed the decorative wrapping and peeled back an inner layer of delicate white paper beneath it. She held up her gift.

"Oh, Jimmy," she said, placing a hand to her chest, "This is nice."

"I thought you might like it," he said, "you loving Christmas so much and everything."

The gift was a framed print of a man wearing a long red cloak, a traveler who'd stopped at an old time inn. The traveler stooped over the shoulder of a young serving maid carrying a drink to a patron. The man held a spring of mistletoe over their heads, and was in the act of kissing the willing maid on the cheek.

"It's beautiful, Jimmy."

"It's a Norman Rockwell print. I found it at the mall. Sometimes I go there when I need cheering up."

She moved her hand across the print, feeling the characters.

"I used to deliver the *Saturday Evening Post* and every magazine cover was done by Norman Rockwell back then. Got some stamps by him, too, in my collection. He was a great artist and had a great talent for capturing generations of Americans doing what Americans do. And this scoundrel in the picture reminds me of my Oliver, that old fox."

"Really? It does?"

"Jimmy, it's too bad you never got to know your grandfather. Oliver would wander around the house at Christmastime and hide mistletoe where I couldn't see it. Then he'd catch me under it, and

131

when I'd tell him he couldn't kiss me, he'd point out where he'd hidden the mistletoe and tell me, yes he could, and that rules was rules. Of course, I'd try to fight him off once in awhile, just to keep him honest, but he always knew my heart wasn't in it. He was clever that way, hiding it above doors, in the chandelier, any place that was above my head. Sometimes he would even hide mistletoe under his cap. He'd call it Daddy's Kissing Cap. And then he'd kiss me and lick his lips and say that one tasted like cherry pie or that one must have been apple cobbler. He always compared kissing to dessert. He was something, he was."

"Where are you going to put my picture, Grandma?"

"I'll put it on the window sill, right where I can see it every day during Christmas."

Jimmy arrived the following day, trailing the aide down the hallway and into his grandmother's room. He grinned as she handed her a bundle of mail.

"You got even more today, Viola," she smiled. "Must be twenty cards in there."

As the aide left the room, Jimmy sat on the bed, looking at the stack.

"What's all that, Grandma?"

"Christmas cards," she replied, reaching for her glasses. "But there's something real funny about all these. I don't know any of these people. I've been getting these cards for a couple of days now."

Jimmy grinned.

"Does it matter that you don't? After all, didn't you tell me once that the deed was more important than the person?"

She grinned.

"Well, I guess you've been paying attention, Grandson. It's funny, though. They're all Christmas cards. People I don't even know are writing me to wish me a Merry Christmas. I'm getting mail from all over the state. See here—postmarked Olivia, St. Cloud, Alexandria, and Litchfield."

"Maybe one of them will be the letter you've been waiting for," he said, winking. "You know, the one in your dream."

She hesitated before answering, her voice dropping.

"No, no, I don't think so."

She opened each card, reading the greetings from each unknown sender. When she finished with each, she handed it to Jimmy.

"This one is from two kids in Litchfield," she explained. "They don't have any grandma or grandpa, so they sent me a card in their place."

She chuckled.

"They want to know if they can adopt me."

"Hey," Jimmy exclaimed, reading one of the cards, "There's a fishing guide in Brainerd who wants to take you out in his boat next summer. No charge, either. Says he'll reserve you a couple of days, but to let him know. He even put a PS, says you'd better bring your mosquito spray—that those skeeters up his way like to carry off little old grannys. How about that, Grandma? You get to go after the big one."

"Pfftt, I'm too old to fish," she replied. "I'm too old for just about anything."

"You're not that old, Grandma," he argued. "And I'm going to prove it to you. How would you like me to take you to the Mall of America tonight and look at all the Christmas lights?"

"That loud old barn," she moaned. "I only been in there once, and it was so noisy and hot that I couldn't wait to get out of there."

"Aw, come on, Grandma, let's go. It's the middle of the week and there won't be so many people there as they'll be on the weekend. You got to see all the lights, Grandma, and the decorations—you know you like decorations. They're beautiful. I'll get Mom and Dad to drive us there."

"You sure you want to do this, Jimmy?" his father asked as they entered the north entrance to the mall that evening. "I mean, you think you can take on this responsibility? Grandma Martin is pretty old, and she shouldn't be getting too excited."

Anna and Viola approached them. Viola sat in a courtesy wheelchair, a cane stretched across her lap.

"Trust me, Dad. I can handle this."

Jimmy turned to Anna as his father shrugged.

"Grandma and I are going to do some mall crawling, just me and her. OK?"

Anna looked toward Jim.

"He wants to show her the decorations," Jim explained

"Well, OK," Anna said reluctantly, surveying the area. "I guess you'll be all right here. But be careful and take it slow. Your father and I will meet you at Lego Land at eight thirty. And don't be late. Grandma Viola needs her rest, you know, and shouldn't be out late. And you've got school tomorrow as well, young man."

Anna and Jim walked away, glancing back as Jimmy headed in the opposite direction, enthusiastically pushing Viola along in the wheelchair. Jimmy wheeled Viola past store after store, each shop window decorated for the holidays. The mall was filled with beautiful trees and magnificent decorations, all ablaze in the colors of the season. Christmas music surrounded them, and shoppers scurried to and fro, searching for gifts as they chatted away. They visited some of the stores, and at one, Jimmy tried on some hats. He placed a red and white striped Cat in the Hat stovepipe on Viola's head and stood back laughing while she protested this indignation. They passed a lingerie shop and Jimmy pointed to a red silk nightgown with pink feathers around the neck. He brushed his eyebrows up and down, urging her to buy the garment; but she waved him off, faking disgust at his behavior. Jimmy took her to a cosmetics shop and convinced her to get a facial until the sight of a heavily rouged woman made her think otherwise. They visited an arcade where he helped her mount a motorcycle parked in front of a large moving screen. The sight of a white-haired grandmother riding a Harley soon drew onlookers who clapped with approval as Viola leaned through hairpin turns and roared down the straightaways. They entered the carnival, the large open area of the mall. Jimmy's eyes widened at the roller coaster ripping through the large enclosure, but checked his enthusiasm. Instead, his attention shifted to the large wheel rising in the distance.

"Hey," he cried, pointing. "I got an idea, Grandma. Let's you and me go on the Ferris wheel."

"I can't climb up there," she protested.

"You afraid?" he teased. "OK, I understand, fraidy cat."

"I am not afraid," she shot back. "I just can't get there."

"Nothing to it, Grandma," he assured her. "I can get us tickets and I'll roll your chair right up to the seat. Then we can see the whole mall from up there. All the lights and all the sights. Come on, it's safe."

Fifteen minutes later Viola found herself seated next to Jimmy, he gleefully watching as the wheel lifted them above the crowd. The wheel rose three stories above the floor of the mall, giving them an excellent view. From her perch Viola could see the holiday decorations and all the shoppers hustling back and forth. The mall had three levels, and each storefront appeared to be trying to outdo the decoration of its neighbors. Jimmy had been right about being able to see everything, she admitted, but as the wheel moved, her seat rocked back and forth more than she liked. The ride slowed and stopped, leaving them dangling at the very top of the Ferris wheel.

"Why are we stopping?" she asked nervously.

"Oh, I asked the man to let us have a minute or two up here," he replied. "Slipped him a ten spot."

"Why, what'd you do that for?" she asked, peering over the side.

"Don't worry, Grandma. You're safe with me."

He pulled a dark cylinder from his coat pocket.

"I've got something for you, Grandma."

She looked in his hand.

"A roll of film? What am I going to do with that?"

"It's not a roll of film, silly. It's just the holder. It's the only thing I could find. But I got something for you inside."

He pried the lid from the top and held it to her nose.

"Just take a whiff of this, Grandma."

She was shocked by the smell.

"That's whiskey!" she shouted.

She looked around to see if someone might have heard, then lowered her voice. "Are you crazy, boy? What are you doing with liquor up here?"

"Shh. Don't be so loud. I didn't bring but a thimble full."

"Where'd you get that?"

"I borrowed it from Dad's liquor cabinet."

"Borrowed it? How do you borrow liquor? Want to get your hide tanned good? You want to get us both in trouble?"

"I did it for you, Grandma."

"For me!"

"Of course for you, Grandma. Who else would I do it for? I figured you could have a Christmas snort, just like you did in the old days when you got cold delivering the mail. It's only a little sip. Come on, be a sport. One day I want to tell people how I rode in the Ferris wheel at the Mall of America with my grandmother and when we got to the top she made a toast at Christmastime. Now that wouldn't sound like such a bad thing, would it, Grandma?"

Seated next to him, she looked like an adorable little doll whose only purpose in the world was just to be hugged. And that's what he did, leaning over to capture her with all the energy of his youth. She thought back to the cold days, when the chilling north wind nipped at her face, and knowing she had three hours left on her route. The fire from a small dram of whiskey had warmed her then. She reached for the small container and peered inside to the small splash of liquid in the bottom.

"Might as well, boy," she said. "Could be the last snort I ever take."

"Don't talk like that."

She held up the container, toasting.

"I guess once the peg's in the hole, nobody cares if it's round or square—just that it's in. OK, this one's for you, Jimmy, and you alone."

She took a small sip. The warm liquor rolled over her tongue, the fumes stealing away her breath.

"Now," she said, "about this one day telling how we rode the Ferris wheel and I drank some whiskey. Don't be telling this just yet, especially to your dad and mom. Or we'll both get a whipping. My Lord, child, what were you thinking about?"

The wheel moved again, around and around, and she felt her heart flutter. The butterflies grew angry; she could feel them. They fluttered again, with pain, needles attached to the wings beating against her heart. She held a hand to her chest and breathed short, hard bursts of air, trying to wart off the stabbing. Jimmy saw her face growing pale.

"Grandma, what's the matter?"

The ride slowed and the wheel came to a halt, their chair the first to unload.

"Heartburn," she replied. "I need to sit and rest for a minute. Just a little rest."

"What's the matter, Grandma? Too much excitement for you?"

Jimmy wheeled her to the food court, where they ate ice cream cones. She felt the stabbing once more, rising and then subsiding. The pain was more intense than ever, but she fought the urge to clutch her chest in the presence of her grandson. The ice cream cooled her throat and the pain went away.

She returned to her room late, happy to be back to her world. She felt better now, but slept wary of a flutter.

Chapter 20

Lois Hernandez addressed her husband as she sat at the kitchen table in the Red Cross shelter, "Why in the world would anyone want to send a Christmas card in two envelopes? Isn't that usually just for fancy invitations?"

Mr. Hernandez sat across from her, reading the card. Two envelopes were laid side by side on the table.

"Dear Friends," he read, "Here's wishing your family happiness at Christmas time. In your time of trial the answers you seek may sometimes come on a wing and a prayer."

"What do you suppose that means?" Mrs. Hernandez asked.

"I don't know," he answered. "But it's signed by somebody named Jenny. Who do we know named Jenny?"

He picked up the smaller envelope.

"And why would anyone put a stamp on an envelope when it doesn't need one? And it's doesn't even have the right postage anyway."

He touched the stamp and it fell from the envelope and dropped into his hand.

"I've never even seen a stamp like this before. It's not even a Christmas stamp."

"Maybe it's not even a real postage stamp," Mrs. Hernandez suggested. "Maybe it's just advertising something."

"I don't know," he answered. "There's just something strange about it all."

He read the message again, staring at the small square of paper resting on his palm.

"On a wing and a prayer," he whispered.

Jimmy visited his grandmother that afternoon, finding her

amidst a stack of cards. Behind her the Norman Rockwell print was propped on the windowsill. He grinned at all the cards on her lap.

"You having fun, Grandma?"

"Lands sake," she answered. "I'm never going to get all these cards read. Look at all these."

"Hey!" he exclaimed, "I got a great idea. Why don't we tape all these up instead of just letting them pile up like that? That way everybody can see them, and it'll dress up this drab old room."

She looked around.

"My room is not drab. You put this tree up, ya twit, and all this other stuff, remember? So you may as well put all these cards up too if you want to."

"Will do, Grandma."

Jimmy left from the room, returning with a roll of clear tape borrowed from the front desk. He began taping the cards to the walls, glancing at the peppermint candies in the cargo hold of the mail truck.

"I see you looking at my candy," she warned. "Stay out of there."

He taped cards below her retirement plaque on the mirror of her vanity. He hung cards on the bathroom wall and on the face of the drawers and closet. Two large cards were awarded a prominent position on the headboard of Viola's bed, where the wood curled forward like a wave. When he finished, he stood back, admiring his work.

"It's so pretty in here now," he joked, "I think I'll spend Christmas day in here rather than dragging you over to my house."

"No you're not," she snapped. "I'm getting fed at your home. Just like Thanksgiving."

John Hernandez squinted, trying to read the phone number scratched on a sheet of paper. Amelia sat at the table, finishing homework while her grandparents sat together on the couch behind her, examining a photograph album rescued from the ruins of the fire. Amelia missed her piano, especially at this time of year when the music she played always brought her family such joy. Mr. Hernandez dialed the phone and heard ringing at the other end.

"Hello," a voice answered.

"Am I speaking to Edward Ramsey?" he asked.

"This is Edward Ramsey speaking."

"Mr. Ramsey, I really hate to bother you so late at night, but the library gave me your name to call about a question I have regarding a stamp. What I have to say might sound strange, but please bear with me until I'm done."

"I'm listening," Ramsey replied suspiciously.

Mr. Hernandez took a deep breath and began.

"Yesterday I received a Christmas card in the mail. At first I didn't think much about it, even though the sender was a stranger to me. And the card came in two envelopes, like a wedding invitation would come in, which I thought was just as suspicious as the words that were written inside. But let me explain how I came to call you, Mr. Ramsey. Inside the large envelope was a smaller envelope, and on it was a strange-looking stamp that fell off when I touched it. Now what is real curious is that this stamp shows an old biplane, kind of a dirty brown, nothing Christmasy about it at all, and I'm just wondering—"

The voice cut him off.

"Who is this and what kind of stunt do you think you're trying to pull?"

"I'm John Hernandez, just like I said, Mr. Ramsey."

"Come on, who is this?"

"I'm John Hernandez, and I'd just like to ask you a question about this stamp. That's all I want."

"OK, Mr. Hernandez, I'll play along for now. But just let me ask you this—what does the value on that stamp happen to be?"

"It's twenty-four cents."

The voice hesitated.

"OK then, Mr. Hernandez, is the—is the plane flying inside of a box?"

Mr. Hernandez studied the stamp in his palm.

"No, it's definitely not in a box. It's more like it's in an oval. It almost looks as if the plane were trapped inside of a mirror."

"And you say it's a jet?"

"No, like I said, Mr. Ramsey, it's a biplane. It's one of those old planes, like they use for crop dusting. And do you know what else—"

The voice cut him off once more.

"Mr. Hernandez, let me ask you something else. Is there anything peculiar about this plane, other than it's a biplane?"

"Why, yes. Something very peculiar. It's flying upside down."

He heard a long silence on the other end of the phone.

"Hello? Hello? Mr. Ramsey?"

The voice spoke again.

"Did this sender say who he was, Mr. Hernandez?"

Mr. Hernandez picked up the large envelope.

"No. There's no return address, but it's postmarked Minneapolis. But I know the sender was female."

"And how do you know that?"

"By the name on the card. She signed it 'Jenny.'"

Mr. Hernandez heard the man gasp, followed by silence. The voice trembled as the man spoke again.

"Mr. Hernandez, I know it's late but I'd very much like to come over and see you. Right away."

Jimmy came down the stairs early, anxious to get the day going, for in two days he would be out of school for the Christmas holidays. His mother and father sat in the kitchen, intently watching the television screen. He poured his cereal and sat down at the table next to them.

"What's up?"

"Just watch," his mother said, her eyes fixed on the TV.

Jimmy studied the small box sitting on the kitchen counter. The face of a female reporter filled the screen, her face stunned.

"I know I'm a news reporter, Tom," she said, "and I'm not supposed to get personally involved with these stories, but I just don't know what to say about this."

"What's going on?" Jimmy asked.

"Listen," his dad replied. "It's all over the news this morning."

The anchorman's face appeared on the screen.

"For those of you who are just joining us this morning, we have a breaking story for you, a story of extreme generosity during this Christmas season. You've all heard of the expression, 'The mail must get through'—well we've got a story about some mail that most definitely did get through. And boy, did it ever. Katherine."

The female reporter's face appeared once more.

"A few days ago many of you will recall that we carried the story of the John Hernandez family of Eden Grove, who lost their house and all their possessions, including their Christmas presents, to a devastating house fire. The family, including the parents of Mr. Hernandez, visiting from Mexico, has been staying in a local Red Cross shelter since the fire. And that's where we're reporting from right now."

"That's Amelia's family!" Jimmy cried.

The reporter continued.

"Late yesterday afternoon, Mr. Hernandez visited the burned out wreckage of his home, and to his amazement found a U.S. mail truck still delivering to his mailbox at the end of the driveway. What amazed him even more was the arrival of a very special Christmas card from someone he didn't know. When he opened the envelope, he discovered a second envelope inside, one with a very strange stamp on it. And, although this stamp at first seemed to have nothing to do with Christmas, it seems that now it has everything to do with it. Let me bring in Mr. Hernandez to tell what happened in his own words."

The reporter motioned and two men stood beside her. Jimmy recognized Mr. Hernandez from seeing him at school but didn't know the other man. Amelia's father was smiling, holding a square of clear plastic.

"We have here with us Mr. John Hernandez and another gentleman, Mr. Edward Ramsey. Mr. Hernandez, can you tell us what happened when you opened this very peculiar Christmas card?"

"Well, when I first opened the envelope," he began, "I found that there was a second envelope inside, like you just said. I opened the inside envelope to find a Christmas card inside."

"And we understand the card contained a very intriguing message, did it not?"

"Most intriguing. It came from somebody named Jenny. She wished us a happy holiday and told us that the answers we seek would come on a wing and a prayer."

"And that was strange to you?"

"Yes, because I didn't know what the words meant. And I didn't know anyone named Jenny. But the smaller envelope had a stamp on it, too, which I thought was very strange, because it wasn't necessary. I mean, why? And it was a strange stamp, like I'd never seen before. So, on a whim, I called the library and they said to contact Mr. Ramsey to ask him about it."

The reporter turned to the second man.

"And Mr. Ramsey, I understand you're quite knowledgeable about stamps. What can you tell us about this particular stamp?"

Mr. Ramsey spoke.

"That's right, Katherine. I am actually what we call a philatelist, which is a fancy way of saying stamp collector."

Jimmy's ears perked. The man continued.

"Mr. Hernandez contacted me late last night with an amazing story about a postage stamp. When Mr. Hernandez called me and began telling me about the stamp he'd received in the mail yesterday afternoon, I thought he was one of my friends, pulling my leg. Then he started describing the stamp in detail, and he didn't sound like he was joking at all. I took a chance and asked him if I could examine the stamp for myself. I visited him here at the Red Cross Shelter, where we are now. To my astonishment he produced the stamp he claimed he had. And it had arrived by mail, just as he'd told me over the phone."

"So what is so special about this stamp?" the reporter asked.

Mr. Ramsey continued.

"Let me explain a bit about his particular stamp by telling you a brief history regarding its origin. On the morning of May 14, 1918 the United States Postal Service issued a special stamp to co-incide with the beginning of airmail service in the continental United States. The stamp design was simple, an oval surrounding the image of the biplane that would carry the mail, flying through the clouds. Unfortunately, in their haste to get the stamp out in time for the inaugural flight, postal inspectors failed to notice that the plane had been printed upside down—"

Jimmy stared at the screen, his spoon dropping into the cereal, clanking against the bowl. Milk splashed onto the surface of the table.

"Hey, be careful, son," his father said.

The man continued.

"—what we call an inverted stamp, and the plane looked as if it were in the midst of completing a barrel roll."

"And what is the significance of the error?" the reporter asked.

"The stamp was recalled," Mr. Ramsey answered, "but not until after some sly stamp collector had spotted the error and pur-chased a hundred of them. The Post Office threatened to confis-cate the stamps, but never did. The plane on the stamp, the one chosen to carry the very first airmail, is an old Curtiss JN-4 bi-plane, perhaps known better as a 'Jenny' and the stamp is known as the 'Inverted Jenny.' Today this stamp is worth well over one hundred thousand dollars, and is very, very rare."

Jimmy's eyes bulged as he choked on his cereal. The man con-tinued.

"And whoever sent this stamp to Mr. Hernandez must have known something about its value. They knew enough to protect it so it wouldn't be damaged or accidentally get cancelled by the Post Office. That's the reason for the second envelope, and probably why the stamp just fell right off, because the sender never in-tended it to stick to the paper. That might have damaged the stamp, decreasing its value. And what really amazes me about all this is, that at a time of year when post offices all over the country are literally buried by millions of pieces of mail, this mysterious person had enough confidence in the United States Postal Service to send this card as just a another piece of mail thrown into the pile."

"And if this story isn't already strange enough," the reporter added, "let me remind our viewers that this letter was delivered to an address without a house on it."

She motioned, and Mr. Hernandez held the stamp to the television camera. Jimmy watched the screen fill with an image he already knew.

"And here it is, folks," the reporter said, "the Inverted Jenny postage stamp. It looks as though Mr. Hernandez and his family are going to have a Merry Christmas after all, Tom."

"And on a wing and a prayer," the anchorman added.

"And all due to the generosity of some anonymous stranger who, coincidentally, goes by the most interesting name of Jenny."

Viola woke from her afternoon nap to find a single envelope lying on the seat of her rocker. She rose and picked up the card. It bore neither a stamp nor postmark, and only her name written on the front. She opened the envelope and pulled out the card. A large Christmas package decorated the front, the box wrapped and tied with a beautiful red bow. Below the package a question mark had been added with a blue marker. The inside held a message:

Dear Grandma,
I guess you were right about God finding a way through doorways.
Merry Christmas,
Jimmy

He arrived half an hour later, smiling at her from the doorway. He walked over to the rocker, bent over, and hugged her.

"Grandma, you're just so darn cool I can't stand it sometimes. You know, Grandpa Oliver wasn't the only old fox in the family."

He'd hung his head as he watched the TV that morning, ashamed at his lack of faith in her, and for thinking that, in the twilight of her years, she had forgotten how to care. Somehow his grandmother had found out about Amelia's plight even before he'd told her about the fire. And though no further words would pass between them, they both knew Jenny.

Chapter 21

Looking at the mountain of cards lying on her bed, Viola said, "So you're responsible for all this, you rascal?" she said, . "I might have known you were involved in this plot somehow."

"You got the letters you said you were waiting for didn't you, Grandma?" he teased, watching a dozen cards slide from the top of the pile and scatter over the bedspread. "You know what they say—be careful what you ask for."

"Yes, but reading all this mail is wearing me out," she grinned, yawning. "But it's a tired I can handle."

Well over two hundred cards had arrived so far, from all over Minnesota, each wishing her a Merry Christmas and seasons greetings. Viola removed her glasses and rubbed her eyes, yawning once more. The room was warm and the rocker lulling, and she closed her eyes as Jimmy watched. She dozed, and the dream came. The hand moved toward the door, pressing against the buzzer. Her face twitched, for the girl stood behind her, blotting out the Christmas tree. She opened the door wider to reach for the letter, and as she did so, the girl's face came into focus. Her features seemed familiar, and slightly older than hers, perhaps twenty. A flawless, milky complexion surrounded symmetrical lips, and soft hazel eyes gazed out from a smooth, rounded nose. Her hair was brown and silky, like that of an angel, and glowed with a faint red hue.

The hand moved toward the two girls, offering the letter. It moved up the front steps and stopped, and she saw her younger self, reaching to accept the envelope. Her body jerked with a stabbing pain, and as the dream shattered, the unknown girl reached from behind her waiting fingers and snatched the letter from her grasp.

Her eyes opened to find Jimmy studying her.

"I'm gonna go now, Grandma" he whispered, bending down to kiss her on the forehead. "You're tired. But I'll be back tomorrow."

The butterflies returned that evening, beating mercilessly against her heart, winged stingers probing for her soul. She woke, gasping for breath, the ticking second hand booming in her ears. The hand appeared later from the darkness. A transparent black glove covered it, a curling forefinger beckoning.

She sat in the rocker when Jimmy arrived the following afternoon, the thick stamp binder resting on her lap.

"Look what I've done," she smiled, opening the book.

Jimmy studied the pages.

"Oh, Grandma, this is so neat. You've put all the Christmas stamps together. Look at all these."

Viola had spent the morning searching the book, rearranging all the Christmas stamps together in the binder. Row upon neatly spaced row of stamps from half a century of Christmas seasons took up two full pages of the binder.

"I thought they all should be together," she explained. "When you open to those pages, you can't help but feel a little bit better, no matter what's happened in your life."

"A lot of memories in those stamps, I bet," Jimmy said.

"Yes, a lot," she replied.

She closed the book and locked it. She handed Jimmy the key, now attached to a leather string.

"I want you to keep this key, Jimmy. Some of these stamps are real valuable, and I don't want anyone opening this book to see them."

Jimmy stared down at the key she offered, accepting it with mixed feelings. He was grateful that his grandmother trusted him, yet at the same time felt regret, for his grandmother had just surrendered her most prized possession and would have to rely on him for its use. He didn't understand why she was giving him the key, but he respected her, anxious to do what she requested of him.

"OK, Grandma," he said, accepting the key. "But I kinda feel like I'm stealing the key to your heart."

She grinned.

"If you only knew."

"I'll wear it around my neck. For good luck. But what are you going to do if you want to look at your stamps and I'm not around?"

"I've looked at them plenty since you came. Besides, if I want to see them, I can just wait for you to get here. You will come, won't you?"

"Sure, Grandma. You know I will."

As he placed the leather string around his neck, she grew somber.

"Sit down, Jimmy, for a minute, will you?"

"Sure, Grandma. Why, is something the matter?"

Jimmy sat down next to her, and she took his hand. He could feel the dry hardness of her skin against his youth, and felt shame at having so much when she had so little.

"No, no, nothing's the matter," she began. "I just get a little nostalgic once in awhile, that's all. I was just looking through my stamps today and remembering back to the war years, when all our boys were off fighting overseas in Europe and the Pacific. It was bad times then, Jimmy, real bad times, but good times, too. Oliver and I stayed here, delivering the mail. But then our boys started getting killed, and their families started getting telegrams about them dying. And weeks later their mothers would get letters from those poor boys, written before they fell in battle. And sometimes I'd have to deliver those letters, knowing that their son was already dead, and when those mothers would meet me at the door and see who the letter was from their hearts would swell, for they knew their boy had risen from the grave. Then I'd have to explain what happened, and the pain of that boy's death would come to them all over again. More than once I'd find myself on the front porch, holding the head of a grieving mother against my body as she mourned her boy a second time."

She felt the head on her shoulder, her hand pressed against the long hair, and the uncontrollable tears of a mother's sorrow soaking her sweater. Jimmy looked at her eyes, glassy, as if tears were about to fall. He squeezed her hand.

"That must have been awful, Grandma."

"It was, Jimmy. I guess I'm telling you this for two reasons. You can't always tell how the cards are going to fall during your lifetime—and you sometimes just have to accept things you just can't understand. And this is a good way of telling you that."

"Sure, Grandma."

She changed the subject.

"Now, tell me what your mother's gonna cook up for us for Christmas dinner."

He told his parents the story that evening at dinner.

"That must have been awful, having to tell someone that," he said.

"I hope you appreciate your Grandma Viola," Anna said. "She's done a lot of good in her lifetime."

Jim glanced at Anna.

"Sure I do. She's my hero," Jimmy replied. "But I wonder who her heroes are?"

Jim spoke.

"She's older than her heroes now, son. Her heroes are all gone. And when your heroes are all gone, you kind of grow to be your own. That's just the way it is."

Jimmy took a bite of peas, wondering why grown ups needed to always speak in riddles.

The rocker creaked against the tile floor as she read from the Bible that night, the pain coming in short bursts. Her heart told her the time was near, and she wondered what it would be like. She wondered what she'd miss most when she got there. She wondered if her skin would grow smooth once more and if her hair would bloom to the vibrant shine of her youth. She wondered if hearts fluttered in heaven, as they did on earth, or if tears ever fell for any reason other than from joy. She whispered another silent prayer for dignity.

She woke later, the pains increasing. The stingers of the butterflies probed deeper into her heart. She took a drink of cold water and returned to the rocker, watching the branches of the bush pressing against the window. The skeleton fingers had vanished, their scratching no longer taunting with fear. She approached the window, her reflection walking to meet her, white, like that of an angel. Her hand pressed against the cold glass, bestowing warmth upon her image. She smiled. She'd wait until morning, she decided, if she could. But for now she would sit in the rocker—and write a letter.

Chapter 22

The students were excited all morning, restless in their seats, for the last day of school before the Christmas break had arrived. Jimmy heard a knock at the door as the class reviewed the answers to a recent test. When Mr. Tyler opened the door, Jimmy was surprised to find his mother in the hallway. She whispered something to Mr. Tyler as Jimmy caught the look of concern on Amelia's face. Mr. Tyler motioned toward him.

"Jimmy," he said. Then, almost as an afterthought, he added, "Better bring your books, son."

Jimmy rose silently, curious about his mother's appearance in the hallway. He gathered his books and left the room without looking back.

"Have a Merry Christmas, Jimmy," Amelia whispered, touching his arm as he walked past her desk.

The door closed behind him and he stood before his mother. A worried look filled her eyes.

"What's the matter, Mom?"

She hesitated, touching his shoulder.

"Jimmy," she said softly, "it's Grandma."

"Grandma?" he asked, surprised. "What's wrong with Grandma?"

She hesitated once more, taking a deep breath.

"Jimmy, it's her heart."

He stared at her, unbelieving.

"Her heart? That can't be. That just can't be. I just saw her."

She squeezed his shoulder.

"Listen to me, Jimmy. Your grandma's sick. She called this morning, and your father and I went down to see her. They've called the doctor—"

"What!"

Tears welled in her eyes.

"It's true," she said. "He's there right now. I came to get you."

The starkness of her words slammed into his mind like a hammer. His books crashed to the floor, the sound echoing through the hallway. Jimmy pulled away from her, racing to the stairs at the far end of the building.

"Jimmy, come back!" she screamed, her arms reaching out.

Flinging open the door, Jimmy flew down the stairs, tearing from the school. The cold wind eagerly attacked him as he breached the outside, for he had no coat for warmth. He rushed through the fresh snow and across the bike trail he'd worn in the grass, now buried by winter. Sneakers crusting with wet snow, he felt a chill against his ankles. He fell once, crawling, and struggled to rise. Panic surged within him, his heart racing as tiring legs weakened in the deep snow, her home seeming more distant as he fought onward. He stopped at the road, lungs burning, and darted across the street, sprinting through the main door of the home. Two nurses stood at the front desk, the same worried look on their faces as he'd seen on his mother's. He rushed down the hallway, trailing dots of white on the carpet. He stopped at her doorway, gasping, but looked in to find his grandmother resting peacefully beneath the covers of her bed. His father was there, as well as another man Jimmy recognized as a doctor by the stethoscope around his neck. His grandmother smiled up at him. Her face ashen, she had the aura of a ghost. Shaken, Jimmy stared at the doctor and back to his grandmother.

"Grandma, what's the matter?"

"It's her heart, Jimmy," his father explained. "She's having heart pains."

"Oh, it's not that bad," Viola, said. "I don't see what all the fuss is about anyway."

"You need to get to a hospital, Mrs. Martin," the doctor ordered. "And as quickly as possible."

"I'm perfectly happy right where I am," she snapped.

153

"You need to listen to the doctor, Grandma Martin," Jimmy's father warned. "He knows what's best."

Anna rushed into the room, her breathing heavy.

"Jimmy," she cried. "Why didn't you wait for me?"

"We need to get Grandma to the hospital," his father repeated, searching Anna's face.

"And I'm afraid I'm going to have to insist that you go, Mrs. Martin," the doctor demanded sternly, staring down at Viola.

"Could you three kindly allow the good doctor and me have a few minutes together," Viola asked, motioning them toward the hallway. "And close the door, will you?"

Reluctantly, the trio left the room, shutting the door behind them. Voices spoke, the words incoherent. The voices grew louder, and Jimmy could hear his grandmother, angry, shouting. The door opened and the doctor appeared, red-faced.

"I've done all I can," he said angrily. "But if you don't get this woman to a hospital, I can't take any responsibility for her health. It's for her own good. I can't do anything more for her here."

He glared at them.

"And I sincerely hope all of you understand the gravity of what I'm saying here."

He stormed out, his neck reddening as he stomped up the hallway.

"Grandma, what did you say to that poor guy?" Jimmy asked, entering the room

"I just told him what was what," she snapped. "That's all. That conceited young pup."

"Grandma, he's just trying to help," Anna explained.

Viola pulled herself up, propping her body against the headboard. Her face grimaced in pain. She looked at her daughter with stern eyes.

"You know what's happening, girl. Don't be denying what's about to go on. I ain't going no place but here. You don't do nothing stupid like calling an ambulance to come and take me away so some doctor can poke away at me and charge a hundred dollars to tell you what you already know. I've been poked at enough. This is my home, and this is where I want to be. Understand me, girl?"

Her words shocked Jimmy, for he'd never seen his grandmother speak to his mother this way.

She wanted to be clearly understood. It would be a waste of her prayers to cart her off to a hospital, like beef to the slaughterhouse. For within her universe, she still ruled.

Anna hung her head, fighting back tears.

"I wish you'd reconsider, Mother. It's for your own good."

"You just let me be the judge of my own good."

Anna moved closer to the bed and leaned down to whisper something to her mother. Jimmy motioned to his father to step into the hallway.

"Why didn't you and mom tell me about this?" he demanded angrily. "How could I not know?"

He felt betrayed, for throughout the many months he'd visited, no one had told him.

"How could she be sick? I just saw her yesterday and she was fine."

His father looked into his eyes.

"We've known for awhile, son. Her heart is weak. It just keeps getting weaker. But this is the way she wants it. She doesn't want to lie around in a hospital bed, too sick to do anything. She always told us that."

"She's just sick, right? She's gonna get well, isn't she?"

"It isn't just that she's sick, Jimmy. She's wearing out."

"What do you mean?"

"The doctor, who just left, said she's probably had a series of minor heart attacks, maybe for months. But she's kept it from everybody."

Jimmy turned pale.

"Heart attacks? How can you hide a heart attack?"

"I don't know. But your grandmother is pretty bullheaded when she wants to be. You, of all people, should know that by now. The doctor says that the attacks were mild enough, but her heart is weak. It's been that way for quite some time. She never let on."

"But what about her medicine?"

"Pills can only do so much, son."

Jimmy shook his head, remembering all the times they had sat there joking; while inside, she felt pain.

"I want you to listen very carefully to me now, Jimmy. I don't know what's going to happen now. I really don't. But I do know she's chosen the road she wants to travel. Let's respect her wish and let her walk down her own path. She wants it like this, Jimmy."

They returned to the room and Jimmy knelt beside the bed. He smiled weakly

"We've got to get you well, Grandma. You know there's mail to deliver. And it's Christmas. Time to be happy."

She grinned weakly, reaching out to take his hand.

"I've done all the walking I'm going to do, Jimmy, I'm afraid. Too bad—my feet could use a good soaking."

He smiled back.

"And I'd soak them for you. Scalded dogs, just like you like."

He suddenly felt guilty, remembering the Ferris wheel. "Maybe I shouldn't have taken you on the—"

She cut him off.

"I had fun. And that didn't do a stitch to bother me."

She grinned feebly.

"And as far as Christmas and being happy, well, I'm about as happy as I could be—all things considered."

They waited in the room while she rested. The second hand ticked unceasingly and time dragged. The room grew crowded and warm. Jim left, returned shortly with a fresh change of clothes. Anna left briefly and returned, her eyes rimmed with red. Jimmy noticed people passing the doorway, each stealing glances at his grandmother, and each looking sad. From somewhere outside came an ominous sound, like the ripping of masking tape. Darkness came to the window.

She lay on the bed later, coughing, covering her mouth with the handkerchief as the phlegm rose from her lungs. Jimmy forced a smile but watching his grandmother's body shake beneath the blankets with each cough, and seeing the stabs of pain in her face, he found himself on the brink of tears. Until this moment his eyes hadn't seen, for his life had been sheltered by the immortality of youth, and knew no other consequence. When he could no longer stand to see her pain, he tore from the room, running down the long hallway and into the darkness of the night. He dropped to his knees in the snow and lifted his head to the sky, gasping.

"Please, God, if you are God, help her. She loves you so."

He raised his arms above his head, upturned palms to the sky.

"Hasn't she given enough, Lord? She's got nothing left to give you. Nothing. You, above everyone, should know that. How could you ask her to give any more? What kind of a God are you, anyway?"

He grew angry, hurling threats toward the heavens with a pointed finger.

"Make her well, Lord, or I will never visit the house of God again. I swear I won't. Do you understand what I'm saying up there? How do you expect me to follow in your footprints when you want so much?"

The snow continued to fall as he knelt low, knees braced against the frozen ground. He lowered his head and began to weep, his body surrendering to the ground. Nearby, the lonely wren, undisturbed by his weeping, slept beneath the bush.

"How could you want her when I need her so?" he shouted, raising his head toward the sky. "Take me, Father, not her. Take me, if you need to take someone. Please take me."

He fell face forward into the snow, sobbing, silent clouds gathering above him.

The long hours passed as they stood guard over her. The night seemed as though it would never end. But then came the dawn.

Chapter 23

The hand that shoved her had been strong and forceful, pushing her onto the crowded sidewalk filled with Christmas shoppers. Over the years, the eyes of the cat had peered out from her dreams, hollow eyes, staring yet not condemning. She had never forgotten the fate of the cat, crushed beneath the wheels of the truck.

She found her balance and turned around as a groan rose from the crowd. The hand that had shoved her hung in the air, its owner spinning into the street, her wide cat-like eyes open in horror as a truck bore down on her. Viola heard the sickening thud of a steel bumper striking a body, and looked down to see the cat on the street. Relieved, she turned and walked into the store.

She relived that moment now, between waves of pain, filling in the missing pieces from over sixty years ago. The hand pushed her onto the sidewalk, into the safety of the crowd. She turned back as the truck raced down the street. She saw the cat cross the road in front of the wheels and shut her eyes, afraid to witness the slaughter. Eyes closed, she failed to see the girl who'd shoved her to safety lose her balance and fall backwards into the street, spinning as she tried to escape the truck. In her mind now the pieces came together, and she stood witness to the young girl's face as tons of steel bore down on her. The girl stared at her, terror-gripped eyes pleading for a mercy that would never come. The truck struck the girl solidly, tossing her body toward the opposite sidewalk as the tire crushed the cat in the same instant. Brakes screeched, drowning out a scream as the young girl's body hurled through the air, time stopping. The wheel rolled over the cat, sharp claws futilely attempting to dig into the tire crushing its body. Bones snapped like twigs beneath smooth fur. The girl's limp body plummeted to the pavement on the far side of the street, hidden by the truck. Eyes opened wide, like those of the cat, and stared blankly into the Christmas sky.

Why the truth was revealed so deeply in the winter of her life was unclear—perhaps the revelation was just her Lord's way of tending to unfinished business. She understood now why the dream had been so persistent with its message through the years. The letter was to have been delivered at that moment of her life, but a stranger had stepped forward to accept it in her place. In pushing young Viola out of harm's way, the unknown girl had taken her place in death. And from that moment, Viola's life had been one of borrow.

The dream made sense now, and could continue.

"How are you feeling, Grandma," Jimmy asked as her eyes opened.

"Thirsty," she replied.

He held her head as she sipped water from a paper cup. He turned away and froze. A priest stood in the doorway. She looked at Jimmy, his eyes lost, searching her face for an answer.

"Grandma, I— "

"I'll let you know," she said weakly.

The priest stepped forward.

The hand moved up the steps, offering the letter. The girl behind her grew transparent, vanishing, and the Christmas tree reappeared, its soft light glowing from the curves of a silver barrette. She stood on the threshold, waiting. The hand reached out to her. She'd always suspected that the bearer of the letter would be Oliver, but as the figure approached, she realized she'd been wrong. She witnessed the dream now from within, from the eyes of her youth, and as the hand approached her, the girl who died saving her was the one who climbed the steps. The girl smiled as she handed young Viola the letter, a gentle, knowing smile. The dream changed, and she found herself looking through the girl's eyes, watching her youthful body turning like the leaves of autumn. Sixty-three years of wear reclaimed her in slow motion, as if someone were applying layers of theater make up. Her body shriveled and bent forward in the doorway, wilting against the unwavering Christmas tree behind her. The young girl continued to smile as Viola's worn hand reached out to accept the letter. She took the envelope and opened it, the girl fading from the dream.

It wasn't a letter that had sought her all these years. It was an invitation. Four simple words called out to her, Come to the Table.

It was time to let her heart relax. She felt it beating within her, like a baby moving within the womb. Gentle hands wove around it, massaging the worn muscle, not to revive it, but to slow it down. A soft, beckoning light radiated from the brass plaque on the wall like the setting of the sun. The clock slowed, second by second, each tick trapped between the finite and the eternal. The soul of the wren rose from the bush, now a dove that disappeared into the sky as a speck of white. She saw Jimmy by her bed, sorrow in his eyes. The wings of the butterflies fluttered, brushing the life from her heart. Surrounded by all that she had been and would become, her dignity had been kept.

She felt the priest's hand against hers and looked down to see the young girl gently tugging her hand. The wrinkles disappeared from her worn hands and her hair grew long and thick about her shoulders, vibrant and flowing. Oliver, in black tuxedo, waited in the distance, top hat tucked beneath one arm. A youth once more, she found herself radiant in a blue silk evening gown, its hem fringed with sparkling silver. She stepped forward, her heart standing alone on the edge of a cliff. With confidence in her Maker, she bestowed upon the physical world the gift of one final beat, and plunged.

Her fingers curled around the letter. And she was gone.

Chapter 24

Jimmy spent Christmas Day at the funeral home. Amelia visited him there, but the secret of the stamp stayed within him, and always would. He knew his grandmother would want it that way. They sat together in silence next to the casket, watching her face. She rested peacefully, as if merely dozing, and her eyes would open to greet them. Her hair had been curled and neatly brushed, and a simple pastel dress covered her, and over it, her postal sweater. On a table next to the casket sat her photo, and next to it, other memorabilia from her days as a mail carrier. The little Christmas tree, its packages dangling from the branches, had been placed on a second table nearer to her head. When Jimmy brought the tree to the funeral home, he made sure his grandmother's star arrived with it; and in doing so, he found the pills.

Those present that afternoon witnessed a sight none of them had ever seen before. A young boy approached the casket late on that Christmas afternoon, staring down in sorrow at his grandmother's body. He pulled a sprig of greenery from his pocket and bent over, holding the mistletoe above their heads. His tears fell upon her face with the gentleness of a spring rain.

"Grandpa Oliver couldn't be here for Christmas, Grandma," he whispered, kissing her forehead. "But I hope a mouse will do."

Amelia stood beside him, strengthening him with her touch, and moving her hand down to hold his.

They followed her coffin up the aisle the day after Christmas, the slow walk, the church silent and solemn around them. Festive holiday decorations adorned the altar and twinkled from the windows, and Jimmy thought how unfair it was that sorrow should come during the most joyous time of year. The key beneath his shirt felt cold against the bare skin of his chest. He glared at the crucifix behind the altar throughout the funeral, angry through his tears.

He didn't know that her life had ended on her terms, with the dignity she had prayed for. It had come at a time of her choosing, when the world, like her, searched its soul for an inner peace.

They followed the hearse to her final resting place next to Oliver's waiting stone, the black iron gates to the cemetery strung with silver garland. Her name and birth date, carved on their stone many years before, looked roughly hued next to the smooth spot of marble that would soon be carved with a last number as well. As they shivered around the cold, open grave, the priest, with his hair blowing in the wind, read the final prayers. Snow fell gently, turning their hair white, like hers.

He visited her room every day for a week, hoping beyond hope that she would be sitting in the rocker one day when he walked in. How does one tell a boy a world he held so dear to his heart no longer has need of him, or no longer is even there? For a week the staff watched him walk the long corridor to the darkened doorway on the left. Day after day he visited the empty room where her sweater had dangled from the hook above the rocker. The room was as empty as his heart, and the slow ticking of the second hand as it journeyed around the face of the clock boomed into the silence around her bed. The nativity scene on the door, the garland around the window, and the rows of cards brought no cheer to him now. He sat among what had been her life, watching from the rocker, lost. The needle of the second hand moved forward, but sometimes, when he heard the ticking, he could see her smiling at him and would bury his face in his hands, the simple words, "Grandma, Grandma," emerging from lips dripping with his tears.

Someone finally worked up the nerve to tell him. They needed the room, and everything had to be packed up. She who had taught him the pain of losing had finally been lost.

He found the letter she had written the night before she died, hidden among the peppermint candies in the cargo hold of the little mail truck. It was addressed to him. He hurried to her grave, to read the letter in her presence. Her headstone jutted from the snow, joined with Oliver's, turning for a moment into the squared face of a postage stamp.

Dear Jimmy,

I want to thank you very much for visiting me here each day over these last few months. Your visits made me feel young again, like I had some value left on this good earth. Oliver would have been proud of you. I'll tell him when I see him that he couldn't have gotten a better grandson. I'm glad you accepted me for who I am, but I'm also grateful you took the time to know me for who I was. When I sit thinking about what I have done with my life and how I have used my time on God's earth, I think I can honestly say that I'm pretty satisfied with what I've done. I'm lucky to have found Oliver, but you already know that. I am satisfied that I brought happiness to people at Christmas with the mail I carried, but at the same time a little sad for those letters of sorrow that I brought as well. The fact that I didn't send them eases my sadness very little. And though I've told you some stories about delivering the mail that weren't as pleasant as I'd like, I'd do it again in a heartbeat.

You know, Jimmy, when Oliver passed on, I turned bitter toward God, even hated Him for a while. Don't you be like that just because I'm gone for now. It's not nice. It was just my turn, that's all. We knew the road would end one day, and except for missing you I'm glad it did. My feet were so weary, Son, but that's something you already knew. And if I had to pick a time to go, I'm glad to go during such a joyous time as Christmas. That may sound strange to you, but it's true. Thank God for youth and old age, Jimmy, for between the two, they'll always be tenderness somewhere on this earth.

I want you to have my stamps. I know you'll take good care of them. You probably know each of them as well as I do. I'll leave you for now, Jimmy, for everything I wanted to say to you has already been said. I guess I just wanted to send one last letter.

With love at Christmas and forever,
Grandma

The Christmas cards continued to come after her death, reminding him of the story of the mothers receiving letters from their sons who'd died in battle. But they opened them, sitting by the tree as the fire crackled, reading the greetings of those who'd taken time to send her cards. They received over six hundred cards and donated them to the home, where the grateful recipients in lonely rooms didn't care that their names weren't Viola. Jimmy tried to visit her grave every day, and he packed up her possessions with his parents, for he no longer had reason to go to the room.

The boy mourned his grandmother for a long time. Christmas came and went, and spring followed the winter. The boy would bike to the top of the hill and look down at the building where his grandmother had lived. His bike trail was exposed as the snow melted, but as the grass grew green over the worn path, the thin link between his life and hers was lost. Sometimes Amelia would join him on the hill, and they would sit and look down from afar, the building growing smaller and more distant. He missed the visits to the small room that had been her universe, where the birds chirped outside the window.

One spring day he took the key from his neck and placed it in a drawer. Summer passed, followed by the chill of autumn. Winter arrived in all her splendor, painting the trees white. And then Christmas.

A bitterness rose within him, building silently as those around him made ready to celebrate the joy. His heart was heavy with her memory. His mother sensed it, for the boy had grown restless and sullen.

"Are you OK, Jimmy?"

He forced out the words.

"Mom, do we have to celebrate Christmas this year?"

His question puzzled her, but she realized now what troubled him. She placed a hand on his shoulder.

"We know you miss her, Son. We all miss her."

"Could we just not have Christmas this year?"

She looked into his eyes.

"Jimmy, Son, listen to me. Christmas is going to come this year, whether you choose to be a part of it or not. Your Grandmother Viola loved Christmas, and she'd want you to honor her by being a part of it."

He rode reluctantly with his father and picked out a tree. When they arrived home his mother had gone to the attic and half a dozen boxes, in various stages of being unpacked, sat on the living room floor. Christmas decorations were strewn everywhere, waiting to be hung. Jimmy helped his father set the tree in its holder, and his mother began decorating the branches. Lights wove their way around the tree and heavy ornaments hung near the end of branches bent them toward the floor. In the background, Bing Crosby crooned an old holiday favorite.

"Now where's that angel?" his mother asked, looking toward the top of the tree.

She motioned to an unopened box.

"I'll bet it's in there. Open that up, Jimmy, and see, will you?"

Jimmy set the box next to him on the couch and pulled open the flaps. He looked down to discover the little mail truck with Postal Service logo.

"Find it?"

Jimmy stared into the box, covering his mouth with one hand.

"It's Grandma's stuff," he blurted.

He reached inside and pulled out the leather book.

"Her stamps," he said. "It's her stamps."

He tried to open the book but found it locked.

"The key," he said, looking towards his parents. "I know where it is."

He raced to his room and pulled the key from the drawer. Returning, he sat on the couch, book on his lap, and unlocked the cover. To his surprise, he found a Christmas card wedged between two pages, its face bearing a red box decorated with gold ribbon. The marked pages opened to the Christmas stamps his grandmother had shown him just before her death. A wave of emotion overcame him as he thought of her.

"I never even got to tell her good-bye."

He studied the page on the right, noting irregular patterns in the rows of little squares. She had been meticulous in her arrangement of her beloved stamps. He knew that, for he had studied the book with her, page by page. And when he'd last seen these pages, the Christmas stamps had been arranged in neat rows and columns. Now they appeared disheveled. He grew irate.

"Who's been fooling around with this book?" he demanded.

His parents stared at him.

"Nobody, Jimmy," Anna replied. "It's yours. And it's been stored since we brought it home. And you had the key."

"Well, somebody's been messing with this," he said. "Look at this mess. Somebody's been moving these stamps around."

He unsnapped the binder, pulling out the plastic sheet that held the stamps. He lifted the page to eye level against the light.

"Well, look at this— "

The colored lights of the Christmas tree lit up behind him as the binder shook on his legs. He sat speechless, staring at the sheet of stamps before his eyes. He lowered his head, fingers pressed against his brow. Curious about their son's behavior, his parents peered over his shoulder to study the page. As the binder slid from his knees to the floor, they too, saw the pattern in the stamps and read the message they carried—Virginia says hello.

Her last words to him, he remembered, had been, "I'll let you know."

Jimmy looked beyond the page, and for a moment, saw his grandmother standing before him, mailbag over her shoulder, waving, her finger pointing to a cross on the flap.

One Year Later...

Jimmy stood on the stage with his parents, gazing out at the crowd. A short distance away, a navy blue cloth concealed a large square propped on an easel. A well-dressed man stood before the podium, waiting. The man bent forward and spoke into a microphone.

"Good afternoon, and welcome. We are gathered here today for a very special reason as we enter this Christmas season. And the reason we are gathered is because of a young man, whose love of someone special in his life caused him to write and tell us about her."

He looked around the room, to the crowd of reporters watching him. He waved a paper in the air.

"In January we received a letter from this young man, and it so moved us that I'd like to read it to you now, in its entirety."

He looked toward Jimmy.

"With your permission, Mr. Paige."

Jimmy nodded. The man began reading.

Dear Postmaster General,

My name is Jimmy Paige and my grandmother used to work for you. In fact, she worked for you for fifty years. She died just a year ago, and I'm afraid that no one will ever remember what a fine lady she was or all she did during her life. She used to tell me how she loved delivering the mail through all those years, especially around Christmas. She's gone now, and others are now doing that job. I just want you to know that she did her job well and that she was proud of those memories. I guess the reason I'm writing is just to tell you about all she did and how much she loved her job, and that her life's work should be more than just a gravestone growing

from the ground. I just think someone should take time to remember her, don't you think?

Sincerely,
Jimmy Paige

The man folded the letter in his hand and smiled at Jimmy.

"Needless to say, the letter caught our attention. We did some
checking and found out that, yes, Jimmy's grandmother, Viola
Marie Martin, indeed delivered mail for the United States Postal
Service for over fifty years. The fact that she so loved her job even
caused our dear Viola to engage in some creative mathematics that
kept her employed a little longer than she might otherwise have
been—but I guess we can't fault her for that. Would that all of us
could find employees such as Viola. And what's even more interesting, Viola Martin worked all those years—that half a century—
those fifty years, with only a few days away from her mail route.
And I guess we'll have to excuse her for missing work, for even as
dedicated as we all know our Viola was, it is somewhat difficult to
deliver a baby and the mail at the same time, even for Viola."

The audience chuckled.

"I would also like to add that her husband Oliver also delivered the mail, but he was a short timer—he only worked for forty-
two years."

He waited for the audience once more.

"We are very fortunate, and let me add grateful, that Mr. Paige
has brought this matter to our attention. And we have decided to
do something about this. Today we are here to honor the memory
of his grandmother's unwavering devotion to her beloved United
States Postal Service. Jimmy, will you step forward, please?"

Jimmy stepped toward the easel, placing his hands on the blue
cloth.

"As we begin this holiday season, we are extremely proud to
issue the Viola Martin Commemorative Christmas Stamp in
honor of this remarkable woman's fifty years of service to the
United States Postal Service."

The man nodded, and Jimmy pulled the cloth away, revealing

a large portrait. Shutters clicked and cameras flashed as Viola Martin, white hair glowing, smiled out at the crowd. The cold blue of the winter's night surrounded her, and trapped in the blue, the Star of Bethlehem shone, its six points reaching out to light the way. Below Viola, a single word had been printed in white, like snow. Christmas.

About the Author

Kevin Prochaska grew up in a small Iowa town, the tenth of thirteen children. He graduated from the University of Northern Iowa with a Bachelor of Science Degree in Geology and from Western Michigan University with a Master of Science Degree in Geology. He worked as a petroleum geologist in the oil fields of South Texas and later throughout the United States and Europe as an environmental geologist. He lives in Kennesaw, Georgia, with his wife Nancy, and children Cassandra, Sarah, Heather, and Thomas.